Being positive is the way forward. Not just in writing, but in life. If you want something, go and grab it. Take the opportunity while it's there, and not regret it after.

(Richard Worth)

A Deadly game

By

Michael Worth

Prologue

Stacey Ashford closes the door of her parent's living room and dims the lights. Sitting down next to her friends Chloe Harper and Emma Lewis, she asks them all if they're sure they want to do this.
With a serious face, Emma looks up and takes a sip of her coke. "Ouija boards are a load of rubbish. I'm sure nothing will happen and we'll all be laughing about this tomorrow".

"Yeah Stacey come on, stop being such a spoilsport and let's get on with it", Chloe replies, folding her arms. "So how does this Ouija board work then?"

Stacey sits with her legs crossed and reads from a piece of paper that she printed out from the internet. "Well it says here we have to have a few candles dotted around the room and be as quiet as we can at all times. So that means no mobile phones or distractions".

Chloe and Emma take their mobile phones out of their pockets and turn them off, before placing them on the table next to them, as Stacey continues explaining the rules of the Ouija board.
"Next, we make sure we have a wooden board with numbers one to nine, a zero, and the complete alphabet from A to Z, and finally, the words *Hello* and *Goodbye*".

"Well we seem to have all that", Emma says, staring at the board on the floor. "Anything else?"
"We have to place a small heart-shaped piece of wood called *a pointer* on the letter 'G', which should move around the board if we get in contact with any spirits. We also have to say a few protection spells, and close the session when we're finished. That's just about it I think", Stacey replies as she puts the piece of paper back in her pocket.

Chloe lights a few candles and spreads them around the edge of the board and around the room, creating a calm ambiance. With the flickering of candle light and the quiet sound of breathing, they each place a finger on the pointer, and wait.

Stacey, Emma and Chloe close their eyes and try to empty their minds of all thoughts. Stacey then says a protection spell aloud.

"In the name of god and all things good, I ask that you protect us from all things evil. I ask that you protect us from harm".

After a few seconds of silence, Stacey and her friends all open their eyes and look at each other.
"We all have to be patient. It may or may not happen straight away, so I've been told", Stacey informs her friends in a quiet calm voice. "Let's again try to empty our minds of all thoughts".
The room is quiet. The street outside is silent. Stacey says another little prayer that welcomes only positive energy. After five minutes of nothing happening, Stacey asks a question to the spirit world, hoping to get an answer.
"Is anyone there?"

After a minute or so, the pointer starts shaking slightly. The girls all look at each other but try to keep their concentration. Slowly the pointer moves to the letters Y, E and S. Much to the shock of the girls they keep going, not quite believing what they're seeing. They all think it's someone else making the pointer move, but carry on regardless.

"What is your name?" Stacey asks in a quiet and calming voice.

The pointer moves slowly around the Ouija board once again, stopping at various letters until it spells out the names, JAMES and HARWOOD. The girls all look at each other a little confused as they really don't know what to make of what's going on. Still thinking it's one of their friends taking the mick.
Stacey asks another question to the spirit in the board. "What year did you die?" After a minute of nothing happening, the pointer slowly moves around the Ouija board again, and starts pointing at different numbers, eventually spelling out the year '1957'. A little

shocked, Stacey decides to ask the spirit one more question before ending the session.

"Which one of us will die first?"

After a few seconds, the pointer starts moving around the board again, but this time at a faster pace. But just before it starts moving to the letters, the living room door bursts open and the pointer flies across the room and hits the mirror on the other side, smashing it, causing glass to shatter all over the floor.
The girls all fall back in shock and look at the door. Standing in front of them is Stacey's neighbour, Ben.
"Hey girls. I was coming home from work and saw flickering lights through the curtains and thought it was some sort of fire or something". Ben just stares at the girls looking back at him. "Is everything all right in here?" Noticing the Ouija board in the middle of the room, he folds his arms and smiles. "I've been there and done that myself when I was your age. I didn't get much luck with it though. I guess I'll leave you girls to it then. Take care girls I'll see you later. Ben says, walking out the door.

Turning back to the Ouija board, Stacey looks up at her friends who all look at the smashed mirror, with the pointer lying on the floor in front of it.
"What happened?" Chloe asks, standing up and walking over to the mirror, and picking up the pointer. "Was that one of you taking the mick?"

Stacey and Emma look at each other, then stand up and walk over to their confused friend stood by the broken mirror.
"It wasn't me", Stacey replies, taking her friends hand in hers.
"Emma did you do that?"

"How could I have done it? It just kind of took off and flew towards the mirror".

Looking at the board then back at her friends, Chloe asks if you're meant to close the session properly.

Stacey answers quietly with her head down. "Yeah you're meant to close it down by saying goodbye or saying a prayer, but Ben walked in and interrupted us so we couldn't do it".

"I still don't know what to make of this whole thing. The wooden pointer hitting the mirror was a little weird, but other than that I'm convinced it was one of you messing around", Emma says with a smile. "Time for a few drinks to lighten the mood don't you think?"

Chloe agrees as she puts the pointer on the table next to the smashed mirror. Stacey stands staring at the cracked reflection in front of her.

After a few drinks and a little laughter, the events of earlier in the night seem to have all but disappeared. Chloe excuses herself as she has to go to the bathroom upstairs.

Walking gingerly up the stairs in the dark, she looks left and right with only the faint sound of her friend's voices in the living room downstairs. Taking each step one at a time, she gets to the top and walks along the landing. Feeling slightly scared, she finds the bathroom, darts inside and closes the door quickly behind her. Sitting on the toilet, she looks around at the well furbished bathroom. Clean and tidy with all sorts of hair products and beauty creams spread across a shelf in front of her. Finishing her business, she starts washing her hands, but as she's doing so she hears a knock on the door.

"I'll be out in a minute". Again a few bangs on the door make her look up in irritation.

"I'LL BE OUT IN A SECOND!" She shouts a little louder.

After she's finished washing her hands, she quickly opens the door. "I told you someone was…."
Without finishing her sentence, she looks left and right in the dark, but can't see anyone around. Walking down the stairs quickly, she stops at the bottom and looks back at the landing. Seeing nothing but darkness, she cautiously carries on walking to her friends in the living room.

"Hey Chloe what took you so long? Did you fall in the toilet?" Stacey asks, laughing at her friend. "Are you all right? You look like you've seen a ghost?"

Emma bursts out laughing, followed by Stacey, and after a few seconds Chloe joins in. "Yeah imagine seeing a ghost. That would be silly wouldn't it?"

The events from earlier in the night have all but been forgotten as Chloe, Emma and Stacey have a few drinks as they laugh and joke the night away.

Putting on her jacket and saying goodbye to her friends, Chloe walks out the door, still a little freaked out from the events of earlier. Waving at her friends as she walks down the garden path, she watches the door close. Turning left out of the garden she gets a fright when she hears a voice from behind her.
"I hope you girls had a good time tonight", Stacey's neighbour Ben says as he takes his dog Stan for a nightly walk around the estate. "That Ouija Board can be very dangerous if you don't use it properly".

"Thanks for the warning Ben, we'll take a lot more care if we do another one tomorrow night. Although after what happened earlier I'm not so sure we will".

Walking away quickly to get his dog back, Ben walks into the road while grabbing his dog Stan by the collar. Waving back at Chloe, he starts walking away.
Chloe turns around and strolls down the street. But just as she turns her head to look back, she hears a horrible screeching sound and a scream. Turning around quickly she sees Ben being hit by a car speeding down the road. He flies over the bonnet and rolls over the roof of the car, hitting the ground behind it with a huge whack. Chloe runs quickly over and screams at the top of her voice at the mess in front of her.

Hearing some commotion outside, Emma and Stacey dash out of the front door to see Chloe with her head in her hands screaming.

"What's wrong, what's going on out here?" Stacey asks, running down the garden path. The sight before her is something she'll never forget as long as she lives.

In front of her on the ground, Ben lay with his eyes open in a pool of blood. His arms and legs broken in multiple places and his dog Stan laid beside him, with his tongue hanging out and his limp body in a pile of blood. Looking around the road, Emma sees the driver of the car with his head in his hands weeping. Neighbours appearing from different houses, shocked at carnage in front of them.

Chloe turns towards Stacey and looks her straight in the eyes. "I caused this. I killed him".

Chapter One

The sound of the alarm clock buzzing at five o'clock in the morning wakes Jack up instantly. Hitting the snooze button he falls back into his bed, pulls the covers over his head and tries to get back to sleep. Ten minutes later the alarm sounds again. Hitting the snooze button once more, he lay staring at the ceiling with a little smile. He's going to start his new job today. As a paranormal investigator.
Jack Harrison has always been interested in the paranormal ever since he was young. Always sensing something is behind him wherever he goes, but when he turns around nothing seems to be there.

Finally getting out of bed, he has a quick shower, puts on a t-shirt and some jeans and walks downstairs. He puts his hand over his mouth, trying to cover a huge yawn from escaping from getting up so early. He stands in the kitchen staring out of the window at the dark cloudy sky, wondering about his new job. It's a lot different to anything he's ever done before.

Jack is twenty-nine years old with short brown hair and a clean-shaven look, as he always tries to look his best in whatever he does. Living in a modest house on a quiet street, he's happy with his life. He worked for a holiday company booking various holidays and short trips around the world for all sorts of people. The money was very good but the days could drag sometimes. Some days you would be busy all day long, while others you would just sit and wait for the customers to come in, but it just didn't happen often enough.

Changing jobs is always a scary and nervous time for anyone. Not knowing anyone and being the new kid on the block. But with some money behind him he decided to follow his lifelong dream and become a paranormal investigator. If it doesn't work out he can always get a job in an office somewhere as he has a lot of qualifications in that area. Sitting down and turning on the TV, he eats his breakfast while watching the sports channel, as the news can sometimes be a bit repetitive.

Finishing his breakfast, he cleans up a few things and throws his dirty clothes in the washing machine. Heading out the front door, he stops next to his car. Looking again at the quiet street he's stood in at 5:45 in the morning, he wonders what his neighbours are doing while he's preparing to start work.

Taking a piece of paper out of his pocket of an email he printed out yesterday, he reads the location out to himself. Once he's memorised where he's going, he starts the car and heads off down the road to start his new job. Driving slowly through the streets he notices how quiet it is. No lights anywhere, no traffic or people, just complete silence. After about ten minutes he comes close to the location where he was told to meet his new workmates. Getting out, he looks around at the area around him. Locking the car, he stands and stares at his surroundings.

In front of him stands a type of hut or shack, with a few windows on the sides and a door on the front. Surrounded by forest on three sides, it looks quite creepy in the dark.
Looking around the area he's not sure what to do, so he just stands still and puts his hands in his pockets and starts whistling to himself. Hearing a voice from behind him, Jack turns around quickly.

"You know you'll scare off any kind of Paranormal Activity if you continue whistling like that".
Walking towards Jack is a guy who seems to be in his early thirties, with a little pony tail and a well groomed goatee beard on his chin. Quickly realising who it is, Jack extends his hand to the man stood in front of him. It's the man he had his quick interview with a week or so ago, Dave Ellis.

"Hey Jack, you must be as mad as me to be out here at this time of the morning", Dave says with a grin.

"I must be mad, it's cold, it's dark and I'm surrounded by a creepy forest", Jack replies jokingly. Shaking hands they have a silent moment, before Dave invites him into the little hut a few metres in front of them.

"Come and meet the team", Dave says quietly, looking around wide-eyed with a serious look on his face. Opening the door, Jack is immediately hit by the warmth emanating from inside. Computers and all sorts of scanning equipment and TV sets fill one side of the hut. Two people are stood watching some kind of monitor, with the other sat in the middle, also staring at the screen.

"Team I'd like you to meet our newest member. His name's Jack Harrison and he's here to help solve the age of old riddle if ghosts exist or not", Dave squeals in a high-pitched voice. Standing just inside the door, Jack smiles and introduces himself.

"I don't know about solving the age-old mystery of ghosts, but I'll help out in any way I can", he says, laughing to himself.

Dave asks his teammates to also introduce themselves.

"I'm John Edwards and I've been doing this ghost hunting for a while but never actually seen anything yet. I'm hopeful though that my first ghost experience is just around the corner. Good to have you on the team Jack, looking forward to working with you".

"I'm Paul Watson and I've only been doing this for about five months but I'm having a lot of fun doing it. You never know what you're going to find. Some of the places we've visited have been really creepy". He Sits back down and opens a notepad and writes a few things down.

"Interesting bunch of people you have here Dave. I think I'm going to enjoy working with them".

"So don't you want to talk to me then?" A female voice mutters from behind John and Paul. Walking towards Jack is a woman he guesses must be about twenty-four or twenty-five years of age. With an average build, wearing thick black glasses and short blonde hair.

Shaking hands for a little longer than necessary, she lets go and introduces herself.

"I'm Laura Jenkins and I specialise in the recording of background noise and trying to filter out voices and other paranormal sounds".

"I think that's called electronic voice phenomenon, or EVP for short if I'm not mistaken", Jack replies, with a proud smile.

Looking at her boss then at Jack she smiles and walks away, but not before turning her head back towards him. "You have a smart one here. Hopefully he lasts longer than the last guy you hired".

"What does she mean last longer than the last guy?" Jack asks, looking at his new boss Dave, who just gives Laura a funny look.

Putting his hand on the door handle, Dave suddenly stops and turns around looking at Jack. "I'll tell you about it later maybe".

Dave opens the door and walks outside, followed closely behind by Jack, Laura, John and Paul. Standing outside they all look into the forest and at the surrounding area before looking at the hut behind them.

Dave breaks the silence with a serious look on his face. "Shall we go and catch some ghosts shall we?"

Chapter Two

"I'm not going with the new guy", Laura moans, as she folds her arms looking a little grumpy. "You're the boss Dave why don't you take him?"

"Laura stop being a bitch and show him the ropes", Dave says, as he drives the van to their first location of the night. Looking a little sheepish, Jack doesn't say anything, he just waits for the pair of them to stop arguing.

"You know if you don't want to go with me, I'll just go on my own. I've done this type of thing before you know", Jack says, trying not to seem like an ass on his first day.

Laura pushes her glasses back up her nose before smiling at Jack. "Fine we'll be partners tonight, but don't get lost or do anything stupid all right".

After ten minutes of driving, they come to a stop near an old playground that seems overgrown. Full of rubbish, broken swings, glass bottles and a rusty climbing frame. Next to the run down playground is a small forest with what looks like an overgrown cemetery beyond it.
Getting out of the van, Paul and John get the equipment they need and put it on the ground next to them while they wait for the rest of the team to sort themselves out. Jack gets out of the van and puts his hands in his pockets and zips up his jacket as the cold is starting to get to him. "You guys do this every day do you?"

Zipping up his own jacket, Dave smiles and puts his hand on Jacks shoulder. "We don't do this every day. Mostly every other day but if something shows up through our various scanners and equipment, we may visit the same location the night after".

"We ready to go then?" Laura moans, with her arms folded looking a little impatient. "It's cold stood here".

Dave explains the rules to the team as he does every time they venture out into the field. "All right just remember to always stay together and keep in contact with your teammate. Be respectful of your surroundings and try not to make too much noise as it's very early in the morning and people are still asleep. Everyone all right with that? John and Paul can check out the forest and make their way towards the cemetery. Laura can you take care of Jack as it's his first time doing this. I'm going to stay in the van and keep an eye on things from here. You all have each other's numbers on your phones so if you get into any trouble just call a teammate".
Sighing, Laura looks at Jack. "Come on then let's go".

Walking into the forest together, Laura and Jack try to be as quiet as they can as they pass various trees, fallen logs and a wire fence that's half buried under leaves and wet mud.
"So what's the plan then?" Jack asks as he looks at the damp forest around him. "Is this place meant to be haunted is it?"
Laura stops in her tracks and looks at her partner. "We talked to a few locals a while back and they said they heard a few noises up here late at night when they were camping. Others said they saw something floating through the woods, while a few said it's all a load of rubbish and all in the mind".

"So you decided to come up here and investigate the area then?" Jack replies, staring at the dark sky above him.
"Yeah, we all agreed it deserved some kind of investigation, so we did a little planning, and here we are", a glum looking Laura explains.

As they walk deeper into the forest, Laura puts her hand out in front of Jack and points to the ground. Bending down she puts her finger over her mouth, telling Jack to be quiet. Whispering as quietly as she can she explains what's going on.

"I thought I heard something in the bush up ahead, we should try to be as quiet as we can for a couple minutes".

After a couple of minutes, Jack looks up as he thought he heard some kind of noise just ahead of them.

"It could have been a rabbit or some kind of rodent".

Everything seems quiet and eerie in the dark forest early in the morning, until the silence is suddenly broken by the sound of Laura's mobile phone going off. Both Jack and Laura jump out of their skins as the tune of a screeching demon can be heard coming from Laura's mobile.

With his heart still pumping fast, Jack looks at his partner with shock on his face. "You're out in the middle of the forest, in the dark, trying to find ghosts, and you have a ringtone like that? Please don't do that again, I nearly had a heart-attack", Jack says, finally calming down.

Answering the phone, Laura smiles while looking at Jack. "Hey Dave, everything's fine here don't worry. But we do have to have a little chat about ringtones and mobile phones going off".

Laughing, Dave agrees before making sure everything's all right. Saying his goodbyes he hangs up the phone.

"Come on new boy let's take a walk through the forest and try to meet up with John and Paul on the other side", Laura says, impatiently.

They walk towards the other end of the forest, always vigilant and listening for strange sounds and watching for anything out of the ordinary. Jack looks at his partner with a strange look on his face.

"What are you looking at?" Laura says, looking down at her feet and back up again. "Did I step in something?"

"You don't like me do you?" Jack says, confused but with a little smile. "I'm not that bad a guy if you get to know me".

Stopping in her tracks, Laura pushes her glasses back up her nose and puts her hands on her hips and stares at the man stood in front of her.

"If I seem a little impatient or mean towards you it's not that I don't like you. I just have a few trust issues, and find working with other people a little stressful. I've been doing this for a while now and I haven't really seen anything that I would consider paranormal so forgive me if I'm a little nasty towards you".

Looking at Laura, Jack smiles. "That's fine don't worry about it. I'm sure you'll see something soon enough if you look hard enough".

John and Paul stand at the end of the forest staring at the overgrown cemetery while waiting for the rest of the team to arrive. Paul puts his equipment on the ground and looks around the area where they're stood. Surrounded by trees, long grass and a few fallen logs.

"Are you all right mate?" John asks his friend.

"Is it me or is it getting cold around here all of a sudden?" Paul asks, putting his arms around his waist.

With both the men stood shivering at the side of the cemetery, a thick fog appears in front of them. They stand still, wide-eyed at the change in temperature and the sudden fog.

"Quick let's set up the temperature meter as we might have something here", John says in a panic.

They reach for the bag with some of the equipment in, just as the temperature drops suddenly again. They both look towards the cemetery, and amongst the fog is what looks like a shadow moving from one side of the cemetery to the other.

"WHAT THE HELL IS THAT". Paul shouts as he picks up a few bags and runs towards the shadowy figure.

"WAIT YOU CAN'T JUST RUN OFF. COME BACK HERE!" John yells, watching his partner disappearing in the distance.

Paul, being excited at actually seeing something, runs straight into the center of the cemetery. Looking around frantically for the figure, he suddenly starts feeling very dizzy. He drops his bags and stretches his arms out wide, quickly finding it hard to breathe. His excitement turns to panic, as he starts stumbling back towards John, who's running in his direction shouting. Paul falls to the ground at John's feet holding his throat.

John bends down to help his friend, and as he does he looks up to see something floating a few metres in front of him. Standing up, he finds himself unable to move out of fear, as the shadowy figure vanishes quickly into the night. As it vanishes Paul starts breathing again, much to John's relief.

Bending down, John picks up his friend. "Are you all right?"
Paul looks up at John before answering quietly and out of breath. "Let's get out of here". Paul starts running towards the forest, with John following closely behind.

"I hear something coming towards us", Jack says in a panicked voice. "It's a figure of some kind".
Running into them is Paul, whose face is a pale white and his eyes as wide as they can go. Following behind him is John, who stops to catch his breath.

"What's going on?" Laura asks, holding onto Paul.

Looking up and looking straight into Laura's eyes, Paul quietly gets out his words.

"I think we saw a ghost".

Chapter Three

Getting back to the van, they all talk about what Paul and John saw near the cemetery a few minutes earlier.

"So what exactly did you see?" Dave asks John showing some concern. "It could have been someone walking through the cemetery".

John looks at Paul, who still seems to be a little shaken up at what he had just witnessed. "The temperature dropped a few times and a dense fog covered the area very quickly. Then out of nowhere some sort of figure moved from one end of the cemetery to the other. Paul decided it would be wise to run towards it and investigate it for himself".

Dave looks at Paul and shakes his head. "Why did you run towards it? You should have stayed where you were and taken some pictures and observed its behaviour. Not gallivant away from your teammate like you did. Now that's out of the way what happened to you?"

"I couldn't move for a few seconds. It was like suddenly walking from a really cold place to a really warm place in the blink of an eye. Quite a calming feeling I have to say. After a few seconds of this, I suddenly had trouble breathing. It felt like the life was draining out of me. That's the only way I can describe it".

"Did you see what it looked like?" Laura asks, putting her arms around herself. "I mean, did you get a good look at it?"

Paul looks at his colleague and answers her in a quiet voice. "It was just this kind of shadowy figure with a bright light surrounding it as it floated around. It didn't seem to notice us until I got near it".

An air of quiet fills the van for a minute or so before Dave decides it's time to call it a night and head for home. The drive back to the hut was one of silence and thinking. Did one of the team actually see a ghost or interact with a spirit of some kind?

Dave drops the team off at the hut and they decide its best they all get some sleep and discuss what happened in more detail later in the day.

"Are you going to be all right Paul?" John asks as he starts up his car. "I can drop you home if you're not able to drive".
"I'll be fine don't worry. A bit of a rest will do us all good after what happened earlier".

John and Paul both leave followed by Laura, who slowly walks towards her car. Turning around she looks at Jack and smiles. "Welcome to the team".

Driving away, she leaves Dave and Jack alone next to the hut. Jack starts walking back to his car but is stopped by an arm on his shoulder. "Laura's not a bad person you know, she's just how shall I say, not much of a team player sometimes".
"Do you really think they saw a ghost this morning?" Jack asks.

Dave thinks about the question for a few seconds before a little smile comes across his face. "I don't know to be honest".

Shaking hands, Jack gets in his car and heads for home. His thoughts full of questions that don't yet have answers. What he does know is that his life just got a little more exciting. Parking his car up outside his house, he unlocks the front door and walks slowly inside.

Closing the door behind him, he feels the hairs on the back of his neck stand on end. Suddenly he's rooted to the spot, unable to move. Suddenly scared of something that might be waiting for him. After composing himself, he slowly walks up the stairs and heads straight for his bed. *What a first day,* he thinks to himself, before falling asleep quickly.

Waking up around ten in the morning, Jack slowly walks down to the kitchen feeling his legs. After walking through the forest his muscles hurt a little bit. Realising he's not as fit as he used to be, he vows to do a little running when he gets the chance. Checking his answer phone for messages and grabbing his keys, he heads down to the local shop to get a newspaper and a lottery ticket. As he's walking down the quiet street, a few kids on bikes whiz past him laughing and joking with each other. A car pulls up next to him and someone inside winds the window down.

"Excuse me can you help me", a female voice asks from the car. "I'm looking for Pendle Street. I was told it was around here somewhere?"

Pointing in front of him, Jack gives the woman directions. "Take the next left at the end of the road and keep going until you come to a mini roundabout. Then take the second exit right and you're in Pendle Street".
"Thank you very much you've been a great help", she says, with a big smile as she drives off down the street.

"You should have asked her out for a drink", a familiar voice says from behind him. Turning around, Jack smiles when he sees an old man stood in front of him. Bryan Walker is about eighty years old but acts more like twenty-five. Always smiling and teasing the women in the local post office.

"She wasn't my type I'm afraid", Jack replies, folding his arms and looking at Bryan, smiling.
"Son let me tell you something", Bryan says in his best old man voice. "Don't be so picky because that girl you just let go could have been your future wife".

"Thanks for the advice Bryan, I'll remember that next time a woman asks me for directions".

"You little scally wag", Bryan mumbles as he walks away slowly laughing to himself.

Buying a newspaper, a lottery ticket and some bottled water from the shop, Jack heads back home to relax a little, before meeting the team again in an hour's time. Sat down in his favourite armchair, he reads the newspaper as he always does in the morning. Even though most of the stories are rubbish and about reality TV, which he hates.

He reads the headlines out loud to himself.

Man still on the run in Camborne. Sarah Jessop tells her story of being kidnapped and held against her will in a cellar for days.

"I know where I WON'T be going for my holidays this summer", he mutters to himself.

Just as he finishes reading the sports section of his newspaper, he gets a text message from Laura, telling him Dave wants to meet a little earlier than planned to discuss the events of this morning. After a quick reply and a quick wash, he heads out the door and into his trusty old car. Putting the music on low, he opens his window as he pulls away. Listening to music on the way chills Jack out a bit as the last few hours have been a bit stressful. Arriving at the hut, he parks his car and heads inside to meet the others.

"Hey Jack how's it going?" John asks as he spins around in his chair. "Dave's running a little late but he'll be here as soon as he can he told me".
Laura walks in the door with a small t-shirt and white jeans on. She puts her bag in the corner and slumps into a chair next to John.
"And how are we this morning?" Jack asks Laura with a smirk.

Laura looks up and drops her shoulders. "If you must know I didn't get much sleep because my idiot neighbours play music all hours of the day. So forgive me if I'm a little cranky towards everyone today".
Dave walks in with a serious look on his face and sits down in a chair next to his desk near the door.

"Right guys and gal, Paul said he wants the day off because of what happened yesterday so it's just us for now. John are you all right with what you saw yesterday?"

Folding his arms and stretching his legs out in front of his chair, he explains what he saw from his perspective.

"We were stood at the edge of the cemetery waiting for Jack and Laura to arrive, and it suddenly got really cold. I mean really bitter all of a sudden. Then a dense fog came out of nowhere around us. Then in front of us, a shadowy figure floated across the cemetery and back a few times. We were both rooted to the spot, until Paul decided to get a closer look. He grabbed his bags and ran towards it.

"What happened to Paul?" Laura asks.

"From what I could see, he had his arms stretched out wide and mumbling to himself, but I couldn't make out what he was saying. After what seemed like twenty seconds, he slowly bent down and started walking quickly towards me holding his throat. The spirit disappeared and we ran into Jack and Laura in the woods".

"That has all the signs of something Paranormal", Laura squeals excitingly, leaning forward towards John.
"We both felt the hairs on the back of our necks stand on end before we saw something float across the cemetery. And I mean ACTUALLY float. It didn't walk. I can say that with 100% certainty that it floated from one end to the other. The feeling was indescribable", John tells the group.
The hut goes silent as they all feel an eerie feeling around them.
Writing a few notes down, Dave looks up and tells the team what he thinks they should do.
"I think we should wait until tonight, then go back to the cemetery and see if we can see the same thing again".
Laura and Jack look at each other and agree, but John seems a little unsure.

"If it's all the same with you guys I'd like to stay in the van when you go to the cemetery. I know I'm meant to be a paranormal investigator but what I saw this morning scared the bejesus out of me".
With a serious face Dave agrees. "It's all right with me. After all we're a team and have to look out for each other".

Agreeing, Laura walks out of the hut without looking at anyone or saying anything. Jack follows behind, looking a little concerned. "Laura wait where are you going?" He asks as she approaches her car. Stopping in her tracks without turning around, she puts her head down and gingerly walks over to Jack.

"Listen Jack, don't pretend to know me or what I'm going through all right. Just leave me alone", she says in an angry voice, before getting in her car and driving away. Leaving Jack standing on his own.

Dave walks out of the hut looking at the car in the distance and then at Jack, a little confused. "Everything all right between you and Laura?"

"To tell you the truth Dave I don't really know. One minute she's happy, and the next minute she's acting like something is really getting to her".

"Don't worry about her. I think she has a few issues in her home life, but doesn't really want to talk about them".

Chapter Four

A few days have passed since the terrible accident outside Stacey's house. Still in shock, Chloe hasn't really spoken about it to her friends or family. She really liked Ben, even though he was older than her, they always seemed to get on really well. Receiving a text from Stacey, which she replies to straight away, they decide to meet at the local coffee shop and talk about what happened.

Meeting Emma halfway, they walk into town. Passing various takeaways and clothes shops, children running around and people carrying various bags of shopping onto the buses dotted around the roads. Seeing a small dog tied up outside the local supermarket, Emma reaches down to stroke it. But before she can get close to it, it quickly stands up growling at her and baring its teeth.

Growling fiercely, it starts backing away, much to Emma's surprise. The girls walk away quickly as they don't want to cause a scene. Looking back, Emma sees the owner appear and stroke the dogs back. After a few seconds it's wagging its tail and jumping playfully with children.
"Well that was strange wasn't it?" Chloe interjects. "Maybe you just have that effect on dogs".
Laughing, the girls carry on to the coffee shop. After a lot of talking about Ben and drinking of coffee, the subject of the Ouija board comes up.

"So are we going to do another one tonight then?" Chloe asks her friends.

"No, I think we should stay away from them for a while now", Emma replies, taking a sip of her coffee. "What did your parents say about the mirror being broken Stacey?"

"Let's just say they were not best pleased", she responds, laughing loudly.

Getting up and leaving the coffee shop, the three girls make their way to the bus stop to catch the forty-One bus back to Stanford road, close to where they all live. Chloe's phone starts ringing, so they all stop outside a computer repair shop and wait for her to finish her call. After a few minutes, Chloe hangs up and they walk away onto the street.

Just as they step away from the building, a massive crash is heard behind them, making them all scream and jump away quickly. On the ground behind them exactly where they were stood, is a large piece of stone that had fallen from the top of the building.

Looking shocked, the girls hurry away and get on the bus as quickly as they can. "What the hell is going on?" Stacey asks her friends as the bus leaves the town.

As the day goes on, Jack does his daily routine of cleaning up and listening to the neighbours arguing about silly things. He calls his mother Janet, who lives in Manchester with his father Steve while catching up on a few TV shows he's recorded.
As night falls, he puts on his extra warm socks and his large jacket. Hopefully to keep the cold out. Walking out the door, he stands by his trusty old car. Very reliable but very old. His friend Lee keeps bugging him to get something a little newer, but at the moment Jacks not budging.
Arriving at the hut, Jack gets out of his car and walks a few metres into the forest. Bending down he tries to be as quiet as he can, listening to all the sounds of the forest at night. From crickets making clicking noises to ruffling of bushes from rabbits.

He finds a log and sits for a few minutes, taking in the calmness and complete silence around him. "*Wow what a creepy forest*", he whispers to himself.
Walking into the hut and sitting down, Jack waits for the rest of the team to arrive. Looking up he realises the door was unlocked. Anyone could have walked in.

Looking around the hut, he see's scanners charging in plug sockets and other various equipment in boxes against the back wall. He also notices piles of books and notes stacked high on the desks. Picking up a diary he finds on one of the desks, he starts to open it, before being told to stop.

"You shouldn't touch things you don't understand", a voice mutters from behind him. Walking over to Jack, Laura picks up a diary and puts it in her handbag she has around her shoulder.
Not someone to get wound up easily, Jack walks over to Laura and stares her straight in the eyes. "I don't know what your problem is or why you hate me but…."

Before he could finish having a go at Laura, the door opens and Dave and John walk in together and sit down at their various desks without saying much at all.

"The plan for tonight is we go into the forest near the cemetery and be as quiet as we can and see if anything happens", Dave tells the group with a serious look on his face. "John and Jack take you're digital cameras and Laura, I want you to take one of our temperature taking meters".
They all nod and agree to the plan. Walking out of the door and making their way to the van, Laura stops and starts to say something to Jack, but stops abruptly and carries on walking. Jack, being a little confused, doesn't say anything, he just follows the team into the van.

Throughout the short journey to the cemetery they all discuss how they'll record any noises they hear and what camera's they will use.

"If we spread out around the cemetery we'll have a better view from all sides", Dave says as he indicates to take the next left at the junction.

Arriving at the cemetery, Dave parks the van and they all get out. John starts talking to Dave while Laura and Jack start walking towards the forest.
While walking with Laura, Jack asks her about her temperature meter, hoping she's in a better mood than she was earlier.

"This device will measure any drop or rise in temperature within a certain distance", she tells Jack, holding the device in the air. "I've had quite a bit of success using this, but never actually seen a ghost using it though".

As the team circle the cemetery in the dark, they all sit and wait for the action to start. Sure enough, the temperature starts dropping. *"Jack look, my meter is telling me something is happening to the temperature. It's lowering quite a bit",* Laura whispers. Jack turns on his digital camera.

"Something's happening", John whispers to Dave, who's taking various photos of the surrounding area.

Sure enough, the temperature drops and the fog becomes thicker. After five minutes of dense fog, it starts to slowly dissipate. With the temperature seemingly returning to normal, Laura stands up and looks around with goosebumps all over her body.
They all walk into the cemetery and meet up near a brick wall. "Well the ghost didn't show", John says, with little emotion, and feeling a bit disappointed.

"Not to worry though", Dave interjects. "We took quite a few pictures so hopefully something will show up on them".

Walking back through the forest, Laura wonders if she's sometimes a little harsh towards Jack. What's happening to her isn't his fault and she shouldn't take it out on him. Looking at Jack walking just in front of her she smiles. Maybe she should get to know him a bit better before judging him.

Sitting in the van, John puts his hand on his chin and wonders why the spirit did not show itself tonight. Maybe it only reacted because Paul approached it. Suddenly he comes back to reality as they pull up outside the hut. Getting out of the van, Dave walks into the hut and picks up some paperwork before walking back out again.

Tossing Laura the keys to the hut, he says he has something he has to take care of and it can't wait. He then gets in his car and drives away.

John, Laura and Jack all walk into the hut and discuss what they saw earlier.

"I think something was there, but it didn't want to manifest itself for some reason", Jack says with his hands in his pockets.

"It did get really cold very quickly, and that thick fog came out of nowhere again", John replies putting a pen in his mouth. "Why don't you and Laura see if you can find out anything about the cemetery. Like how long it's been there and how old are the residents that are buried there", John asks.

"I think that's a great idea", Jack says in an excited voice. "A little research will help us bond as a team. Isn't that right Laura? It'll help us get to know each other a bit better as well".

Laura can't help but smile at Jacks enthusiasm.

John picks up his camera and puts it in his pocket. "I'll inform Dave later of your little field trip into research". Walking out the door he says his goodbyes and drives away quickly. Leaving Laura and Jack alone in the hut together.

"So where do you want to start with the research then?" Jack asks, with a smile. "I'm guessing it's a bit late now, but we could start early tomorrow morning if you like?"

"Yeah that sounds like a plan. What time were you thinking of in the morning?" Laura asks.

Jack stands up and zips his coat up. "I can pick you up around ten in the morning if you like?"
Before Jack can carry on speaking, Laura goes very quiet and tells him not to worry about picking her up, she'll meet him at the sun dial in the city center around ten.

Jack walks out the door and watches Laura lock the hut and walk towards her car.

"You all right Laura?"

Before she drives off, she looks back and smiles at Jack. "I'll be fine don't worry".

Paul relaxes at home after his day off. Seeing something floating across the cemetery really got to him, and nearly having his breath taken away made him realise he should be more careful. Still not sure what happened to him, he stares out the window at the world outside.

"Darling you coming up to bed, It's getting late?" Paul's wife Susan says from the bedroom upstairs.

"I'll be right up".

Turning off the TV, he walks upstairs and into the bedroom, but nobody's there and the bed's still made. A little confused, he walks out of the bedroom onto the landing and shouts Susan's name, but he gets no reply. Seeing a shadow appearing from the spare room, he jumps suddenly when Susan appears in front of him.

"You all right dear?" Susan asks, showing some concern, and putting her hand on his shoulder.

"I'm fine, just feeling a little weak that's all, I just thought…It doesn't matter darling lets go to bed". Seeing his wife asleep next to him Paul stares at the ceiling from his bed. Unable to sleep.

Chapter Five

Stacey wakes up to bright sunshine outside. Birds singing and the unmistakable sound of the ice cream van rolling down the street. Looking at her clock she notices it's only 8:45. *The ice cream man didn't waste any time did he.* She thinks to herself.

Pulling the covers back, the first thing she notices is she's completely naked. "I must have forgotten to put anything on last night", she says, giggling to herself.
Getting out of bed she stands on the scales and weighs herself, closing her eyes before looking back at the scales. Happy with her body, she combs her blonde hair and puts on some tracksuit bottoms and a t-shirt.

Hearing a knock on her bedroom door, she hears her father tell her that her breakfast is ready, so she tells him she'll be down in a minute. Deciding to have a shower after breakfast, she opens her bedroom door and walks down the stairs, hoping to see her breakfast already made for her. Instead, she's greeted by silence. No breakfast smells or parent's around anywhere. Walking into the living room and checking the back garden, she can't see anyone anywhere. Even the car is gone from the driveway outside. The place is empty.

Walking into the kitchen she sees a note on the table.

We've gone to visit your Nan across town because she's still very ill. We had to leave early to beat the traffic, so we'll be home sometime later.
Have fun dear.

"So who knocked on my bedroom door then?" She says out loud.

Suddenly the house becomes a very creepy place to her. Stood still, she looks around at the clean and tidy kitchen. Thinking what she heard was in her mind, she walks up the stairs and takes her clothes off before she gets into the shower. As she's washing herself, the bathroom starts to steam up. Humming to herself she relaxes and lets the water run over her body.

As she's washing her hair she gets soap in her eye and tries to rub it out, but it doesn't help. Pulling back the shower curtain she reaches for the towel to dry her face and get the soap out. As she reaches for the towel, she feels a hand grab her wrist. Screaming and jumping back, she falls over onto the shower floor. Unable to see what's going on in front of her.

"SHIT WHAT'S GOING ON?" She shouts as loud as she can. "WHO'S THERE?"

Curling up in the corner with the shower still running, she waits for whoever it is to grab her again. After five minutes she calms herself down and turns off the shower. Cautiously looking around the bathroom she doesn't see anyone, so she grabs the towel and races towards her bedroom.

Slamming the door behind her and breathing heavy, she stands as still as she can, hoping whoever's in her house has gone. With her eyes darting left and right and her ears trying to listen for any kind of sound, she slides down the door and puts her head between her knees. Feeling herself starting to shiver from still being wet, she dries herself off with the towel and puts on a t-shirt and some jeans and sits on her bed. Wondering what to do next, she grabs her mobile phone and she calls her friend Emma.

Emma answers her mobile phone to the sound of Stacey crying.

> "Is everything alright Stacey? Speak to me, what's up?"
> "Emma I think someone is in my house".
> "What do you mean someone is in your house?"
> "I felt someone grab my wrist when I was in the shower".
> "Stacey, stay where you are, and I'll be over in five minutes".

Grabbing her jacket, Emma runs out of her front door and down the street in the direction Stacey's house. Running as quickly as she can, she crosses the road and past the chip shop until she comes to a small bridge over a lake that runs between the neighbourhoods. Feeling herself tiring, she breathes a sigh of relief when she can see Stacey's house in the middle of a row of houses. Walking quickly up the garden path, she grabs the front door handle and pulls it down. Pushing the door open, she notices how deathly quiet it is inside.

Walking inside, she feels the hairs on the back of her neck stand on end. Looking left and right, she doesn't see anyone. Trying to stay aware of what's around her, she gradually makes her way upstairs towards Stacey's bedroom, while being as quiet as she can. Reaching the upstairs landing, she stands still, thinking she may have heard a noise. Tapping softly on Stacey's bedroom door, she waits for her friend to respond. After waiting for all of ten seconds, she grabs the handle and pulls it down.

Opening the door gently, she peeks around it to find Stacey curled up in the corner with her head between her knees. Walking over she reaches out to touch, her but stops suddenly.

"Stacey are you all right?" She whispers as quiet as she can.

"WHO'S THERE?" Stacey screams as loud as she can.

Upon seeing her friend, Stacey jumps up and throws her arms around her. "I'm so glad you're here Emma I really am. I was grabbed in the shower by someone, so I ran as fast as I could in here and waited for you to arrive".

Relieved Stacey is all right, Emma closes the bedroom door and sits on the bed next to her friend.
"We have to do a search of the house to see if anyone is still here", Emma says, looking at Stacey who's still shaking with fear.

Standing up, Emma opens the bedroom door and takes a look outside. With Stacey following closing behind, they walk across the landing checking all the possible places someone could hide. Slowly walking down the stairs together, looking every which way for any kind of movement. They then search the kitchen and the living room but don't find anyone anywhere.

After all the rooms had been searched, they sit in the living room and go over what had happened earlier.
"Are you sure someone grabbed your wrist in the shower? Could it have possibly been your imagination?"
"I'm positive someone grabbed my wrist as I reached out for a towel", Stacey replies, a little confused. "I also heard my father call me for my breakfast but I couldn't find him anywhere".

"Stacey what's going on?"

Both the girls look around at the quiet house, before both coming to the same conclusion, but not sure they should say anything.
"Are you going to be all right here on your own, because I have to sort my flat out. It's a complete mess", Emma asks Stacey, who looks visibly calmer than she did earlier.

"Yeah I'll be all right now. When you've gone I'll lock all the doors", Stacey says to her best friend.

After some encouraging words, Emma waves goodbye as she walks down the garden path and off down the street. Stacey stares at her friend until she can't see her anymore, then walks back into the house, locking the front door behind her. Suddenly the house seems creepy again. Walking upstairs, she looks at herself in the mirror and smiles.

"All these strange happenings must be in my mind. I've been a little stressed lately. Maybe an early night will do me some good".

Walking out of her bedroom, she walks timidly into the bathroom to wash her face in cold water. Filling the sink, she bends down over it and throws some cold water over her face. As she stands up, she gets the fright of her life when she sees what's written on the mirror in front of her.

Chapter Six

As Jack relaxes in the garden drinking a cup of tea and listening to the neighbours arguing again, he hears his mobile phone going off. He reads a text message from Laura telling him she'll be a bit late as she has a few things she has to do first. Putting some decent clothes on, he looks in the mirror and ruffles his hair, because he can't be bothered doing much else with it. Hearing his mobile going off again, he answers it and instantly gets annoyed that it's another cold caller wasting his time trying to sell him windows and doors.

"Listen I don't want any more windows or doors, and my roof doesn't need resurfacing all right, now go away".

Putting the phone down, he smiles to himself as he likes having a go at these companies selling rubbish to him. After having a little snack and answering a few texts from friends, he makes his way into town. Driving along a dual carriageway at a normal speed, Jack spots someone coming out of a junction, but they don't stop. They race out in front of him causing him to break sharply and sound his horn to stop them from hitting him. The guy in the car starts shouting and swearing at Jack, who winds his window up as he doesn't want any trouble. After a few seconds, the guy just drives off, so he carries on into the city to meet Laura. After waiting for ten minutes, Jack starts to walk away from the sun dial because he doesn't think Laura's going to show up.

A voice from the bench near him makes him look up. Laura's sat smiling at him with her handbag on her lap.

"How long have you been here?" Jack asks, folding his arms.

Laura stands up and walks over to Jack, putting her handbag over her shoulder. "About ten minutes I think. I was seeing how long you would wait for me".

"Did I pass your little test?" Jack asks, with his arms still folded. "I was freezing my ass off while you were sat watching me".

Laura turns around and walks away slowly with a little smile, as she pulls her handbag over her shoulder once again. "Come on lets go".

Walking alongside Jack, she asks where they should go first.

"I emailed the local paper and asked if I could look over a few things from their archives, and they politely said that they didn't mind as long as we were quiet", he replies with his hands in his pockets.

Laura starts walking a little faster. "That's great. It's going to rain in a minute though, so we had better get a move on".
Walking into the local newspaper building, they're met by Steve Harris, the managing director. Who then invites them into his office and asks why they want the old archives of the town. Laura explains that being paranormal investigators, they have an interest in a certain part of town that they believe to be haunted. Not sure whether to believe them or not Steve sits back in his chair and folds his arms. "I don't believe in all that ghost haunting stuff. I think you're wasting your time, but as long as you're respectful and quiet, I'm willing to let you go through our archives".

After spending an hour looking over various slides, newspaper articles and drinking a lot of coffee, they decide they're getting nowhere fast. Jack looks up and asks Laura what happened to the other member of their group that she mentioned a while back.

Laura takes a sip of her coffee before explaining what happened.

"He was called Danny and he seemed like a decent guy. I only knew him for a couple of months but he was one of those people you couldn't help but like. Really friendly and someone you could trust if you got into trouble. Then one day we went out on a field trip to some old bomb shelters that we heard were haunted. Danny and I checked out one side of the bomb shelters while Dave and Paul checked the others.

It was really dark in those old shelters, but Danny decided to wander off in front of me on his own. I heard a loud scream then Danny came running past me. After I caught up with him I noticed his face was pale and his eyes were as wide as they would go. I asked him what he saw but wouldn't tell me. He left the group within a few days and we haven't seen him since".

"Did you go back in and try to investigate what he thought he saw?" Jack asks, holding his coffee with both hands.

Laura stares at Jack before answering. "No, we didn't go back in; we got out of there pretty quickly. Shame, as I liked Danny, we got on really well".
Taking another sip of her coffee, Laura looks up at Jack and sighs loudly.
"I suggest we go and visit the cemetery and see what the oldest gravestone is and work from there".
Jack puts some papers back into the folders and agrees. "We do seem to have wasted our time here. Not to worry though, at least we tried".

Thanking Steve Harris on their way out, they make their way to the cemetery in the hope of finding something that will shed some light on the strange happenings of a few nights ago. While driving to the location, Jack wonders about Laura. They seem to be getting on well as a team, but there's something up with her that he can't put his finger on just yet. She always seems to be on edge.
Parking the cars, they approach the cemetery. Laura walks through the gate, that creaks as she pushes it open. "It looks very different in the day time, less creepy".

"So what are we looking for exactly?" Jack asks.

Laura takes off her jacket and puts it on the grass. "We're looking for names on gravestones. This cemetery seems to have been abandoned a very long time ago. Maybe the oldest name and the newest name might give us a time frame as to when it was first, and last used".

After spending some time looking around, they write down a few names and dates and meet up on a grass verge overlooking the overgrown park.

"Do you ever think about the future Laura?" Jack asks, staring up at the sky. Looking sheepish, Laura just looks at Jack for a second and then turns away, not sure how to answer him.

"Do you plan to do this forever, or do you have a dream to do something else?" Jack asks a still puzzled looking Laura. "Are you all right?"

"Jack, I'm just not feeling sociable today to be honest. Can we just get on with what we were doing?"

"Yeah of course we can", Jack replies, without questioning his partner.

Sharing the information they collected, they start telling each other some of the names and dates.

Jack starts telling Laura what he found first.

"Dennis Anders died 1878, Steve Moon died 1900, Michelle Smith died 1912 and the final one I have is Fred Tumble who died in 1934. That's the newest date I could find".

Laura shares her information with Jack.

"Anna Ruth died 1890, John Earl died 1896, Earnest Elmer died 1923, Mattie Mae died 1917. The final name I have here is from a man called James Harwood, who died in 1957".

Hours later, Dave and John are sat in the hut talking about cars and finding the best ghost videos and images on the internet.
"Some of these look really fake", John says, chuckling at some of the more fake looking videos.

"There are some genuine scary photos out there, but you just have to know what's fake and what's real", Dave replies, watching another video.

Sitting back on his chair, John asks Dave what he thinks of Jack. "He does ask a lot of questions but he seems to enjoy what he's doing as well. It'll be interesting to see if he can turn Laura into a team player".

"Now that's something I'd like to see as well", John replies, taking a mouthful of his coffee.
Hearing the door of the hut open, Dave smiles when he sees Laura and Jack walk in holding a few pieces of paper and a box of donuts. Putting the donuts on the table, Laura slumps down in the chair and takes a deep breath.

"Everything all right?" Dave asks, taking a donut out of the box.

Laura just smiles and takes a donut. "Just feeling a little tired that's all".

"So what did you find on your little field trip then Jack?" John asks, taking another sip of his coffee. "Anything interesting to report?"

"We wrote down the names on the gravestones that were in the cemetery. Although a lot were really faded from years in the sun and rain, we managed to get most of the names right I think", Jack tells his teammates. "Now we're going to find out about those people through the internet or head back down the newspaper office and see if they have anything on them. It's a long shot but we'll give it a go".

"Before you go wondering off again, I have a few things to tell you first", Dave says, while looking at a piece of paper aloud.

"We have a new case to start on soon and a couple places I want to check out. But before that, I think we should all as a team go and see how Paul's doing. He told me since the incident in the cemetery he hasn't been feeling very well. I've given him some time off to sort himself out, but it would be a nice surprise if we paid him a little visit and cheered him up".

They all agree on Dave's plan to visit Paul. But first they all decide to go home and relax for an hour before heading out again. Dave drives John home while Laura and Jack go their separate ways.

Jack gets home and throws his keys on the kitchen table before slumping on the sofa in the living room. *Working in an office is a lot easier than chasing ghosts around*, Jack thinks to himself. Although his new job is a lot more exciting than the last one.

Hearing a knock on the front door, he gets up and casually walks towards it. Opening the door he sees his ex-girlfriend Sandy stood in front of him, who left him for a younger man about two months ago. With an average build and long brown hair, she knows she can wind Jack around her little finger very easily.

"What do you want Sandy I'm kind of busy?"

"I just came over to see how you were doing that's all".

"I'm doing fantastic thanks, now can you go away", Jack says as he tries to close the door. But Sandy stands in the door, stopping him from closing it fully.

"Come on Jack can't we talk about this like adults?"

Opening the door wide, Jack folds his arms as a big smile appears on his face.

"Talk like adults? It wasn't me who was sleeping around was it?"

Not sure what to say, Sandy walks away before looking back at Jack. Looking a little sad at Jack's response. She starts to talk but gets interrupted.

Closing the door quickly, Jack stands on the same spot for a minute, before walking upstairs and having a quick shower.

Laura opens her front door to find her boyfriend Alan asleep on the sofa with empty beer cans and empty crisp packets scattered all over the floor. Sighing, she starts to clean up the mess but a hand grabs her arm and stops her.

"Have you made me any food yet? I'm starving", Alan asks, pushing rubbish and crumbs on the floor. "I'm going upstairs to the toilet, and when I come down I expect my food to be in front of me". Slumping his way upstairs, he belches, before going into the toilet and slamming the door. Looking around at the mess in her living room, she sighs, before picking up the cans and the rubbish and putting them in the bin.

Putting some chips in the fryer, Laura sits down on a stool in the kitchen and starts reading a magazine on health and beauty. Seeing how happy some of the women look with smooth silky hair, she puts her hands through hers and smiles. Hearing Alan coming down the stairs, she puts his chips on a plate with a tray, so he can then eat them in the living room as he watches the TV.

Upon seeing just a plate of chips and some sausages but without no steak, Alan looks up at Laura and frowns.

"What do you call this? Where's my steak?"

"Alan we don't have any steak. I've been working all day, why didn't you go to the shop and get some?"

"I'm not eating this crap", Alan moans as he throws the meal into the bin before stomping out the kitchen. "I'M GOING TO THE PUB", he shouts at Laura, before walking out of the house.

Laura sits down on a stool and watches Alan walk across the road and out of sight. Putting her arms on the table, she puts her head down and starts crying to herself. She wonders what she has done to deserve being treated like this.

Chapter Seven

Staring straight at the mirror in front her, Stacey is scared to move a muscle. Written on the mirror in what looks like blood, is the word '*die*'. Completely afraid to move, she stands and stares at the word in front of her.

Thinking what she should do next, she looks left and right and bolts out of the bathroom door, down the stairs and out of the front door. Stopping at the end of her garden path she looks back at the house, before quickly running down the street. Upon reaching a block of flats, she runs up two flights of stairs until she reaches Emma's flat. Knocking on the door as she bends down to catch her breath.

Emma answers after a few seconds to see her friend Stacey with a pale face and panic in her eyes. Bending down to her level, Emma asks her what's up.

"You look shattered, what's going on?"

"I saw something in the bathroom mirror", Stacey says, still panting and trying to catch her breath.

Emma puts her arm around her and invites her inside to try to calm her down. Stacey sits down in the living room while Emma makes some tea for her in the kitchen. Looking around the room Stacey notices a few photos on the walls as well as a games console underneath the TV. As the kettle's boiling, Emma comes into the living room and tells Stacey that she just sent a text message to Chloe, and asks if she could come over straight away.

Finishing changing her hair colour from light blonde to brunette, Chloe combs it and admires it in the mirror. Smiling at her new look, she puts the used hair dye packet into the bin and walks downstairs to the kitchen. Where she finds her phone that's been making a noise for the last minute or so.

After answering a text message from Emma, she puts the phone back on the side and trots back upstairs to put some decent clothes on. Halfway up the stairs she hears a loud knock on the front door. Looking over her shoulder she sees a shadow through the frosted glass. As she's walking down the stairs she hears another knock, this time even louder than the last.

"I'm coming, I'm coming", she moans, getting a little annoyed".

Not sure who's on the other side, she grabs the door handle and pulls the door open wide.

"I told you I was…." She stops mid-sentence when she sees no one is stood in front of her. Looking left and right, she looks a little puzzled as she swore someone was stood there a second ago. Stepping out into the garden, she looks left and right again, but doesn't see anyone around. Not thinking too much more about it, she closes the door and walks upstairs to get changed. Putting on her red t-shirt and blue jeans, she smiles at her new hair colour in the mirror. Grabbing her mobile phone and putting on her jacket, she walks down the stairs and out the front door. With the sun out and a slight breeze in the air, she strolls down the road humming to herself. Waving to her neighbours, she continues until she gets to Emma's flat. Knocking on the door she hears a voice telling her it's open and to come on in.

"Hi Stacey how are you doing?" Chloe asks her friend as she sits down on the sofa.

Not really saying anything, Stacey shows a weak smile and waits for Emma to finish making the tea before telling Chloe what's been going on this morning. Sitting down and passing each of them a cup of tea, Emma looks at Stacey and asks her to tell Chloe what she had seen this morning in the mirror.

Taking a sip of her tea, Stacey puts the cup down on the small table in front of her and puts her hands in her lap. Chloe looks between Emma and Stacey not sure what's going on.

Stacey starts telling her friend what happened.

"I was having a shower and got soap in my eyes. I then reached for a towel but I felt someone grab my wrist. Not sure what to do I phoned Emma. She came over and calmed me down a little. When she was gone, I decided to throw some cold water on my face. I went into the bathroom and bent down to splash my face. But when I looked back up, I had the shock of my life. The word "die" was written on the mirror in what looked like blood or some kind of red paint".

Chloe looks at Emma with panic in her eyes, not sure what to say. After a full minute of silence, Chloe finally speaks up.
"Are you sure that's what you saw? You weren't seeing things or anything like that?"

Sitting forward on the sofa, Stacey shakes her head and looks down at the floor and back up again.
"I wasn't seeing things Chloe, it was clear as day, written on the mirror in front of me".

After a little discussion, Emma and Chloe decide the best thing to do is to go and see it for themselves. Locking the flat behind her, Emma catches up with her friends and together they walk in the bright sunlight. As before when the girls went into town, a stray dog sat next to some bins jumps up at them and growls as they pass. Only to lay back down once they've gone past.

"What's that about?" Emma says, looking around at the dog.

"Your hair looks nice". Emma tells her friend. "Definitely suits you". Chloe puts her hands through her hair and smiles. "I like it as well, maybe I'll change it to red next time".

Stacey thinks for a second and has an idea what might be happening to her and her friends, but doesn't want to share it with the others yet. Approaching her house, Stacey gets out the house keys to unlock the door, but quickly realises it's unlocked. Not sure if she locked it as she ran out earlier, she doesn't think anything more about it. Walking inside, all the girls feel a sudden cold rush over them just as the front door slams behind them, causing them all to jump forward in fright.

"WHAT THE HELL WAS THAT!" Chloe screams, looking back at the door.
Looking slightly scared, the girls walk up the stairs cautiously and stand outside the bathroom door. Looking at each other, Chloe decides to be the first one to open it. Very slowly the door creeps open. Looking at the sink with the water still in the bowl, they all stare at the mirror above it.

"I don't see anything written on the mirror Stacey", Chloe says looking confused. "Maybe it was all in your mind. You have been a little on edge lately".

"Yeah Stacey come on, I think you need to spend a few days away from here and clear your mind", Emma replies, folding her arms.

Agreeing, Stacey and the girls decide a camping trip away somewhere would be good. They've all seen strange things lately but haven't told each other. Maybe the fresh air of the countryside will clear their minds. After much discussion about the location, and how long they'll be away for, they agree to drive out into the woods and set up a couple of tents and to chill out for a while. Emma and Chloe will bring the tents while Stacey agrees to bring the food and drinks.

Chloe starts packing a few bits and pieces in a large bag. A few clothes and some bottled water and maybe a little make-up. After five minutes, she's ready to go on a camping trip with her friends. Walking downstairs, she puts her bags by the front door and waits for the other girls to arrive. Sitting on the sofa, she looks around her empty flat and feels slightly nervous. With a silence in the air and the ever so soft sound of the wind outside, she closes her eyes and takes a deep breath. Thinking about what's happened to her and her friends lately, she wonders if it has something to do with the Ouija board they did.

Looking straight ahead and concentrating, she's suddenly brought back down to earth by a knock on the door. Like the last time she heard a knocking sound, she can see a shadow through the frosted glass in the middle of the door. Not sure what she should do, she stands perfectly still. Walking slowly towards the door, she grabs the handle and pulls it open. Again with no one there she starts to close the door, until out of nowhere Emma appears in front of her. Jumping back suddenly, she sees the shock on Emma's face.

"Are you all right Chloe? Sorry if I scared you, your neighbour wanted a quick word with me".

"Yeah I'm all right. Just let me catch my breath a bit".

After picking up Stacey, they head through the town and out into the many fields and forests that lay on the outskirts of the town. Passing horse riders and many caravan sites, they turn off the road and onto a dry muddy path. Driving for ten minutes they come to a clearing, where they park the car and wander off into the forest looking for a place to camp out.

Chapter Eight

After Laura replies to a text message from Dave, she gets a few things together and drives towards Paul's house. Stopping at the traffic lights, she looks to her left and sees Jack looking at her with a smile on his face. Sticking her tongue out playfully, she looks straight ahead, and as the lights change she slowly drives off. Parking just down the road from Paul's house she gets out of the car and walks towards Dave and John who are sat talking in a car.

"Hey Laura, how you doing?" John asks from the passenger's seat of Dave's car. "Any idea where Jack is?"

Sitting on a small wall next to the car, she smiles and looks down the road. "He's on his way now I think".
Parking behind Dave's car, Jack gets out and walks towards the team. Nodding at John in the passenger seat, he gives a thumbs up to Dave, before standing in front of Laura and smiling.

"Everything all right Laura?" He asks, folding his arms. "Yeah everything's fine. Just a few things going on that I need to sort out that's all".

Dave and John get out of the car and stand with Jack and Laura next to the wall. John tells Laura he tried phoning Paul this morning a few times but couldn't get an answer. Walking down the street, the team follow Dave until they get to the gate outside Paul's garden. Laura looks at Dave and smiles before she walks past him and knocks on the door. Not getting an answer, she cups her hands to the glass on the front door but can't see much.

Laura pulls the handle down, and to her surprise, it's unlocked. Pushing open the door, she pokes her head in and shouts to see if anyone's home.

"HELLO, ANYONE HOME?"

Not getting any response, she pushes the door open wide, and the team follow her in. Closing it behind him, John walks into the living room and gets the fright of his life. The white leather sofa is covered in blood. The light blue carpet is also covered in blood. In the middle of the floor laying on her back with her eyes open is the body of Paul's wife, Susan.

Hearing a sudden shout from the living room, Dave, Jack and Laura all rush in to see what's going on. Upon seeing the dead body on the floor, Laura puts her hand over her mouth in shock.

"MY GOD WHAT THE HELL HAPPENED IN HERE!" She shouts in a panic.

Jack and Dave stand rooted to the spot. Shocked at what they're seeing in front of them. Fully clothed with her hands by her side and her legs spread out straight and her eyes open, Pauls wife Susan has a long slit across her throat.

Walking backwards slowly step-by-step, Jack wonders upstairs and takes a look around. Various blood prints can be seen on the walls. Walking into a bathroom that should be pure white is stained by the colour red. Blood prints on the bath, sink and mirror.

Walking into the spare room, Jack doesn't spot anything out of the ordinary. Just a few boxes, a cupboard and an old exercise machine. Walking onto the landing he stops in his tracks. He can hear a faint noise coming from the bedroom across from him. Pushing open the door gently, he stands back in shock at the sight in front of him. Walking backwards he walks down the stairs and into the living room. Seeing Laura sat on the sofa and John and Dave stood out in the garden, he calls them all back inside.

"I've found Paul", Jack tells them in a quiet voice.

Without saying anything else, he turns around and quickly walks up the stairs with Laura, Dave and John following closely behind.

Before they walk into the bedroom Jack turns around and faces his friends.

"Are you sure you want to see this? It's not a pretty sight".

Dave and John nod their heads while Laura just stares at the door in front of her. Turning around, Jack pushes the door open wide to reveal a sight nobody should ever have to witness.

Laura again puts her hand on her mouth in shock and walks out of the room where she stands on the landing. Dave and John look around the room, who are also in shock at what they're seeing. The ceiling fan whirls slowly above Paul's swinging body. A noose sits tightly around his neck with a knocked over chair on the floor beneath him.

Written on the wall on the far side of the room is the word '*die*' in large letters in blood. Walking back into the room, Laura once again looks at the body and the writing on the wall.

"I'm going to call the police", Dave says, walking out of the room and taking his mobile out of his pocket.
John also decides there isn't a lot he can do, and walks towards the back garden, followed by Laura and Jack. Standing and staring out at nothing in particular, John looks at his friends and sits on the wall next to them.

"How can something like this happen?" John asks Laura. "He was always such a calm and relaxed person. He loved his wife and loved his job. He had so much going for him".

Laura replies in a quiet voice. "I don't know. We were only speaking to him the other day and he seemed fine. Nothing to suggest anything like this would happen".

Jack doesn't say anything as he doesn't really know Paul that well. He lets his friends do the talking while he listens to what they have to say. From what he remembers, Paul was a nice guy who seemed to be enjoying life. Hearing sirens coming down the road, the four friend's walk back through the house and meet up with Dave in the front garden.

After talking with a lot of the police officers and ambulance men, Dave gets told that he and his friends are allowed to leave and go home.
"I think we need a bit of time to ourselves after what we've been through today", Dave says. "A few days off for all of us to get our thoughts together are needed".

Laura, John and Jack agree, and after a bit of hugging they all go their separate ways. Sitting alone in her car in her driveway, Laura starts crying. She thinks of all the good times she shared with Paul.

Not sure whether he should call Laura and make sure she's all right, Jack sits on the sofa alone thinking about the last few weeks of his life. He's met some really nice people and got a job he enjoys doing. Putting his mobile on the table, he takes another sip of his beer. The one question that keeps coming up when thinking of Paul is why? Why did he do what he did to himself and his wife? Was it even him that did it? After a couple more beers he makes his way upstairs. As he reaches the top, he looks into the darkness. Thinking he has seen something, he walks into the spare room. Only to be met by silence and darkness. Getting into bed, he lays thinking about the events of today. Such a waste of two lives.

As night falls, Dave sits in his living room wondering what to do. Paul was his friend and now he's gone. After talking to John on the phone until late, he walks up the stairs to his bed. Kissing his girlfriend Anne goodnight, he lays with his eyes open not sure he wants to carry on doing what he's doing without his friend.

Chapter Nine

Finding a clear spot amongst the trees, Chloe, Emma and Stacey all drop off they're various camping equipment and sit on the dry ground. Looking at the sky, Emma spots a few dark clouds approaching, so she starts putting up her tent. Stacey then wanders off into the bush to have a look around, while Chloe also starts putting her tent up.

Walking a few yards away from her friends, Stacey follows a footpath until she comes to what looks like an old shack that has seen better days. With all four walls and the roof seemingly still intact, and a fallen tree resting on the top of it. It looks perfect for somewhere to hide out if the rain gets too heavy. Walking further on, she spots an overgrown playground that doesn't seem to have been used for some time. With a rusty climbing frame and rubbish everywhere, it's not somewhere you'd want to be in the dark, she thinks to herself.

Hearing a noise behind her, she stops in her tracks. With everything she's seen lately she doesn't know what to expect anymore. Running out of the bush comes a stray cat that spots Stacey straight away. Stopping suddenly, it stares at her, then it runs away into another bush.

Slightly relieved, she decides she's done enough exploring and heads back to her friends.

"Where have you been?" Emma asks, with her hands on her hips. "You shouldn't wander off like that without telling us".

Nodding, Stacey agrees with her friend. "Yeah sorry about that. My adventurous side in me came out and I did a little exploring".

"What did you find?" Chloe asks, poking her head out of her tent. "An old playground that doesn't seem to have seen much action for a while, and an old shack. I'm sure I saw something else out there through the trees, but I decided to come back. I think we should go and check it out".

Nodding in agreement, they disappear into their tents and get a few items together for the short trip across the forest. They grab some food and drink and other various pieces of equipment they think they might need.
Zipping up the tents, they start walking through the forest. The sound of birds and the rustling of trees surrounds them with every step they take. Insects climbing up branches and broken logs scattered everywhere. It's a peaceful and serene place to walk, they all think to themselves.

"So how's your hairdressing job coming along Stacey?" Chloe asks, taking a sip of her water.

"Yeah it's going really well, and people seem to like what I do. I've only been doing it for a few months, but I'm enjoying it. It's only part-time at the moment but hopefully it'll be full-time soon".

They all walk into the middle of the overgrown playground and look around at the state it's in. Chloe walks towards the climbing frame but decides it's too rusty and dirty to climb. Chloe takes a few photos with her camera as they all head in the direction of the small shack. Approaching the old shack they stop outside of it and look around.

"Wow what a creepy place this is", Emma says, putting her hands in her pockets. "Not the ideal home is it".

Laughing, Chloe puts her hand on the door and pushes it open gently. Much to her surprise the door creaks open slowly, revealing the inside in full view. An old wood fire sits on the far side of the shack with rotten chairs, branches and leaves scattered about its floor. The ceiling looks sturdy, but with the log on top of it outside it doesn't look like it would last in a big storm. A table stands in the middle of the room with a few empty plates on it. Screwed up newspapers lay in one corner and an old bird cage in the other.

Chloe picks up one of the newspapers and reads the date. '2006' is written just under the headline. *'Britain in Economy panic'* "This has been here for a while then".

After looking around and picking up various things, the girls walk back outside to complete silence. Standing next to each other they look at the forest around them. No birds are singing, no insects clicking or trees rustling. Standing concerned, Stacey feels a cold breeze pass her head from behind her.
Turning around quickly she looks in the direction of where the breeze came from. Seeing Stacey turn around, Emma and Chloe do the same. In front of them just past a few trees and bushes, stands what looks like an old cemetery. Walking past the trees and through some of the bushes, they come to a stop near the overgrown cemetery.

"This place looks really old", Chloe says, walking towards an entrance partly covered by some overhanging trees.

Following behind their friend, Stacey and Emma walk in different directions and look at the various gravestones dotted around the area. The gravestones are surrounded by a part rusty wire fence and some overhanging trees which give it an eerie feeling. The girls walk past a few of the gravestones and read the dates and names on them, surprised they're still readable after all this time.

As Chloe walks through the grounds, she thinks she spots something in the forest to her left. Turning quickly, she thinks she saw a shadow passing through the trees. But as she does so, she trips on a piece of wood on the ground and falls over. She then ends up landing in some old newspapers stuck under some branches. Hearing a scream, Emma and Stacey come racing over to see what's happening. Finding their friend on the ground with a pained look on her face, Stacey asks Chloe if she's all right, before holding out her hand to her friend.

"Yeah I'm all right, I just tripped on some rubbish that's all".

Taking Stacey's hand she gets back to her feet and is immediately shocked at the name on the gravestone in front of her.
The name on the gravestone says. "JAMES HARWOOD. Died 1957". The girls all look at each other, not sure if it's a coincidence or possibly the same person who they had contacted through the Ouija board.

A small smile appears across Chloe's face. "It's just a coincidence. Isn't it?"

"Yeah course it is", Emma and Stacey say at the same time.

The lack of any sounds around them, the girls decide it's time to start walking back to the tents before it gets too dark. As the suns setting over the tops of the trees, the girls find some food and sit around a small campfire that Emma had made a few minutes earlier. Passing some food around, Stacey looks at her friends and asks the question that's been on everyone's mind for some time now.

"Do any of you think that all these strange things happening to us are to do with the Ouija board we did a while back?"
Chloe looks at Emma and nods her head. "Yeah I do. The bricks falling off the building and the knocking I had on my door the other day tells me something's wrong. I'm not sure if I believe it's the Ouija board though".

"Dogs don't seem to like me much anymore for some odd reason as well", Emma responds quietly, taking a sip of water. "Stacey you've had some weird things happen to you haven't you?"

"Yeah I have. The hand grabbing me on the wrist and the word '*die*' written on the bathroom mirror remember".

Putting her hand in the air, Emma puts a finger over her mouth before telling her friends to be quiet, as she thinks she has heard some rustling in the bushes behind them. Looking left and right, the girls start to panic as the wind starts getting stronger, and clouds appear suddenly in the sky. Grabbing a few items from the tents, the girls start running towards the old shack a few yards away. The rain starts to get harder and harder as the girls struggle to see what's in front of them. Finding the shack, they all run inside and close the door behind them.

The sound of heavy breathing and panting can be heard throughout the dirty shack as the girls try to catch their breath. Hearing the rain lashing outside they hope the shack will last the storm. Hearing a loud crash outside they all stand up and move quickly to the door just in case the ceiling gives way. After fifteen minutes of continuous wind and rain, it suddenly stops as quickly as it had come around.

Opening the door, Emma walks outside followed by her friends. Standing outside they look back at the shack and are surprised to see that it had withstood the storm they had just been in. Walking back through the woods, they can see drops of rain dripping off leaves, and the unmistakable smell of wet mud and trees after a big rain fall.

They all stop abruptly when they get to their little campsite. The crashing sound they had heard earlier was a massive tree coming down across their tents. Looking in disbelief, they walk over to the crushed tents and pick up the bits and pieces they can find that belongs to them.

Chloe looks at her friends in disbelief. "Imagine if we had decided to stay in the tents instead of running to the shack earlier, we would all be…"
Before she can finish her sentence, Emma puts her hand up and stops her from talking anymore.

"Don't say it Chloe. I think we all know what you're going to say".

"I don't think we should hang around here much longer", Stacey says, looking around at the wet ground and feeling a slight breeze in the air. "It's getting dark very quickly and if we don't move now we're going to get lost trying to find the car".

Hearing a strange noise behind them, they all quickly walk back through the forest, hoping they find the car quickly as the dark is approaching very fast.

Walking close together, they keep alert to any kind of movement around them. Hearing footsteps behind her, Stacey starts running, followed by her two friends. Before long, they're all running as fast as they can straight ahead, hoping to find the car before whatever had made the noise catches up with them.

Finally seeing the car in the distance, Emma takes her keys out and presses the button that unlocks all the doors. A mad flashing of lights can be seen all around them, as the three girls dive into the car and drive away to safety. Looking left and right out of the windows, the girls finally calm down as they leave the wooded area and onto the long stretch of road leading back into town.

Pulling over on the side of the road, Emma cuts the engine and lets everyone catch their breath.

"Stacey can you pass me your bag so I can have a drink please", Emma asks. "I think I dropped my water when we were running through the forest".

Passing Emma her small bag, Stacey sits back in her seat, still a little shaken from the events of earlier. Seeing Emma pull a piece of paper out of her bag and look behind her, Stacey looks at Chloe then back at Emma.

"What's wrong? What is it?" Chloe asks, looking worried.

Emma puts down the bag and holds up a white piece of paper with the word 'die' written on it in blood.

Chapter Ten

After a couple of days rest from work, Jack feels a lot better about things. Thinking about the brief time in which he knew Paul, and how happy he seemed. It does strike him as strange that he would do something so savage to his wife.

Just as he's about to leave to go swimming, he receives a phone call from Dave, asking him if he's all right to meet with him and the rest of the group in about twenty minutes time at the hut. Agreeing to meet them, Jack puts his swimming stuff away and heads out to his car.

After the short drive to the hut, he parks his car and then waits in his seat for a few minutes. Unsure what to do or what to say to his friends when they start talking about Paul. Getting out of his car he walks slowly towards the hut, not sure if he wants to carry on being a paranormal investigator.

Opening the door, he spots Dave sat at his small desk writing something down on a piece of paper. On seeing Jack, he smiles and asks him to sit down somewhere. As he sits down John walks in, followed by Laura. After they've taken their seats, Dave puts his pen down and stands up.

"Before we get down to business, I would just like us all to bow our heads in memory of our good friend Paul".

Laura, John, Jack and Dave stand up and bow their heads for a minute or so in respect for Paul. Sitting back down, Dave looks around the hut at his friends and work colleagues.

"It's nice to see you all again here as a team. What happened to Paul and his wife was tragic and heart breaking. We don't really know the truth yet and I suppose we never will, but his memory will always be of a kind, fun and smart person".

"Have the police released any more information yet?" John asks quietly from the corner.
Dave looks at John without much emotion. "No they haven't said anything yet".

"I'm not good at these sort things so I'll just say that he was a good friend and I'll miss him a lot", Laura says quietly from her desk.
Jack nods his head and agrees with Laura. "I only knew him briefly, so I didn't know him as well as you guys, but he seemed like a decent guy".

After a minute or so of silence, Dave looks up with a serious face. "After a lot of thinking I've decided I'm going to carry on being a paranormal investigator. If any of you want to leave I won't hold it against you. The last few days have been tough on all of us".

John looks at Jack, who in turn looks at Laura. Standing up, she looks over at Dave and the rest of the group. "I think I'm speaking for all of us when I say that we want to carry on doing what we've been doing".
Smiling, Dave nods his head. "I'm glad you're all going to carry on. It's what Paul would've wanted".
After talking about how they will go about things now Paul's gone, they decide the best thing to do is to get out there and investigate the paranormal.

"I have a few cases we could work on but I'd like your opinions on what we should do next", Dave says, looking at a few pieces of paper. "We have an old woman who's convinced that her ex-husband is haunting her. We also have a newlywed couple who've just moved into a house that they say is haunted by something.

Looking at the group, Dave asks what they all think would be the best job to take on. Laura smiles and picks up the piece of paper on Dave's desk and passes it to him. Looking at the paper he smiles and stands up.

"I think we should see what the old woman has to say, and to see if she really is being haunted by her ex-husband".

After getting a few notes together, they all head out to the van and make their way across the town to the old woman's house. As they approach the street, Dave slows down and parks the van a few houses away and gets out, followed by the rest of the team. Standing and looking at the house, John gets out his camera and starts taking a few pictures.

Dave knocks on the door as Jack joins him. After a few seconds it slowly opens and a little old woman peaks her head around the door frame.

"Can I help you?"

"I'm Dave, this is Jack, and we've come to see if we can help you with your unusual problem".

Opening the door wider, the old woman smiles and lets Jack and Dave inside. She then leaves the door slightly ajar for the others to join them, after they've taken more pictures.

Walking through the house, Jack senses a very homely smell about the place, which is typical of an elderly woman's home. With plants on tables and photos on the walls, he can't help but smile as he thinks of his own parent's house. The living room has a soft blanket covered chair sat in front of the fire, as well as a few chairs dotted around the place. Above the fireplace sits a picture of the woman and her husband. Sitting next to each other, Jack and Dave start to ask a few questions to the old woman about the ghost she thinks is haunting her.

"How do you know it's your husband haunting you?" Jack asks in a quiet voice. It could be any kind of ghost".

Sitting back in her chair, she puts her hands together in her lap and thinks for a second.

"Well dear, I can smell his aftershave sometimes when I'm wondering about".

Dave and Jack look at each other and back at the old woman. "Sorry we didn't catch your name".

"My names Edith Cook, and I'm eighty-two years old", she replies with a loving smile. "I lost my husband Walter, about five years ago".

"I'm sorry to hear that", Jack says.

After talking to Dave and Jack for a while about her husband, and what she gets up to on a daily basis. She then stands up slowly and waddles to the kitchen. Hearing the kettle boiling, Jack stands up and walks around the room, before turning around and looking at Dave.

"Do you think she's really seeing her dead husband, or is she just wishing it's her dead husband?"

"To be honest Jack, I'm not really sure, but it won't hurt to take a look around for a while will it?"

"Yeah you're right. We'll finish the tea Edith's making, and then we'll take a look around and see if she has something here". Finishing their tea and biscuits, Jack and Dave walk upstairs with Edith, who slowly walks into the spare room and stands against the back wall. The room has a set of drawers against one wall, as well as a few boxes stacked on top of one another on the opposite side. A lamp also swings above them, as a double window looks out onto the street.

Edith leaves them alone for a while as John and Laura walk in and start taking photos of the various parts of the room. Dave's temperature meter, doesn't pick up any changes until John tries to speak to Edith's dead husband Walter.

"Walter are you here?" John asks the empty room.

"Keep talking", Dave quietly mutters, as his temperature meter shows a slight change.

Dave presses the record button on a small audio recording device in his pocket, hoping to hear any sounds from the spirit, if it's there.

"Do you smell that?" Jack asks Laura. "I can definitely smell aftershave in here".

"You know what? I can smell it as well", Laura responds, looking at John and Dave who nod in agreement.

After ten minutes, Dave points to his temperature meter and gives the thumbs down. Then they all walk out of the door slowly, closing it behind them quietly as they do so.
Finding Edith sat in her chair drinking tomato soup, they quietly walk to the front of the living room by the fire. Dave then explains to her what they were doing upstairs.

"We took a few pictures and things like that, so after we find out what we found we'll let you know".
"Thank you very much for helping an old lady out. I miss Walter every day, and if he is here, I would like to say a final goodbye, and to show him the light if I can".

After leaving the house and making the short journey back to the hut, they all go inside and sit down. John turns the heater on, as it's starting to get a little chilly at this time of the year. Inserting the memory card into the computer, Laura and the team all wait patiently as the buzzing sound of the hard drive fills the air. After a few seconds, the screen fills with a mountain of pictures. Some of the images are good, while others not so much.
Searching through the various pictures of the garden and the other rooms of Edith's house. John points to a certain photo and asks Laura to enlarge it a little. As she presses a few buttons, the spare room comes into view.
John, Jack and Dave all lean back and stand up staring at the screen. Laura can't take her eyes off of the picture either.

"Well I didn't expect to see that", Dave says, staring at the screen.

Chapter Eleven

After a nervous and silent trip home Stacey, Emma and Chloe all walk into Emma's flat and sit down. Not sure what to say, they just look around the room in complete silence. Emma puts her hands in her lap and leans forward.

"I think we really need to talk about what's been going on lately". The girls all look at each other and nod their heads slowly. Sitting back and folding her arms, Chloe tells her friends what she thinks is happening.

"I think it has something to do with the Ouija board we did. Ever since we did it, all kinds of strange things have been happening". Stacey stands up and walks around the room nervously, not sure whether to believe Chloe or not.

"We have to be honest with each other here, because I'm scared shitless at what's been going on", she says nervously, as she sits back down in front of her friends.

"I can honestly say it wasn't me moving the pointer around the Ouija board", Emma replies looking across at Chloe.
"It wasn't me neither. I always thought it was one of you two doing it", she responds. "You mean something actually came out of that board?"

Stacey twiddles her fingers nervously. "We didn't close the session down properly because Ben came in and broke our concentration. Then the pointer flew across the room and smashed the mirror. I don't think any of us could have done that".

"So what about the word *'die'* that seems to be following us around a lot lately. Also, what about the tree falling over our tents? As well as the storm coming out of nowhere. Then there is Stacey getting totally spooked out in her house. I believe in coincidence, but this is getting a little too scary for me", Chloe says quietly.

They all decide to go home and carry on with their normal routine, but if anything does happen then they're to contact each other straight away. Saying her goodbyes, Chloe walks out of the flat and across the road towards her own home. Walking up the stairs, she puts the key in the lock and turns it slowly. Opening the door, she walks in and closes it behind her. Looking ahead of her, she sees nothing but the sunset coming through her living room window, illuminating the hall in an orange glow.

Putting the kettle on, she opens the fridge and picks up the bread and butter to make herself a sandwich. Just as she starts buttering her bread, her mobile phone starts ringing. Not recognising the number, she hesitates whether to answer it or not. Picking it up cautiously she presses the answer button and puts it to her ear.

"Hello?"

Hearing a slight shuffling on the other end, she pulls the phone away from her ear and looks at the number again. Putting it back to her ear, she again asks who it is.

"Hello who's this? I'm going to hang up now".

She hears the shuffling getting louder before it quickly stops and the phone goes silent. Then a voice starts talking quietly on the other end.

"You killed me Chloe. You ended my life".

Looking shocked, Chloe doesn't know what to say, she just stares at the phone in her hand in disbelief.

"Who's this?"

"You killed me Chloe and now you're going to pay".

The phone goes silent for a few seconds, before a blood-curdling scream causes her to drop it on the floor. Standing and staring at the phone, which has a creepy sound coming from it. She quickly bends down and presses the disconnect button. Still standing and staring at the phone, she hears a knock at the door that causes her to jump backwards. Seeing a figure through the frosted glass, she slowly walks towards the door. Putting her hand on the handle she stops suddenly and looks at the figure.

"Who is it?"

The figure doesn't say anything, it just stares at Chloe through the frosted glass. Not sure whether to open the door, she takes her hand off of the handle and turns the key, locking the door. She then asks again, who's there, in a frightened voice.

"If you don't answer me I'm not letting you in".

After a silence, Chloe starts backing away from the door. She starts walking slowly backwards up the stairs, trying not to trip up. Suddenly the figure behind the door speaks.

"It's me, Ben. You killed me Chloe and you're going to pay".

Screaming at the top of her voice, she darts upstairs and runs into her bedroom, slamming the door behind her. Breathing heavy, she looks around her room for something to jam the door shut with. Pushing her bed against the door, she sits in the opposite corner with her knees pulled close to her body.

"What's going on?" She whispers in a terrified voice.

After Stacey leaves, Emma feels alone in her flat. Picking up her phone she starts to dial Chloe's number but stops halfway. Thinking that she'll probably be busy doing something and that she doesn't want to be disturbed.

Walking upstairs and into the bathroom, she then takes off her clothes and looks at her trim body in the mirror. Smiling, she walks into the shower and then realises she doesn't have her towel with her, but she just carries on anyway.

After a long hot shower, she gets out and walks to her bedroom, and dries herself off. She then puts on her tracksuit bottoms and starts gently brushing her damp hair in the mirror. Thinking she has heard a noise coming from her living room, she puts down her brush and walks away, and down the stairs into the living room. But her reflection doesn't move, it just stares at her walking away.

Walking into her living room, she sees a picture on the floor that looks to have fallen off the wall. Picking it up she notices a big crack through the middle of the glass on the front. The picture is of her, Stacey and Chloe from last year when they went to a theme park for a couple of days.

Hearing her mobile phone ring, she looks up and starts walking towards the kitchen, oblivious to the figure stood behind her. She turns around quickly thinking she saw something out of the corner of her eye. Seeing nothing there, she picks up her phone and answers it. Hearing a shuffling sound on the other end she looks confused.

"Hello, is anyone there?" Emma asks.
After a few seconds of silence, Stacey starts speaking.
"Hi Emma could you come over I have something I want to talk to you about, it's urgent".

But before Emma can reply, her phone goes dead.

Putting her mobile in her pocket, she runs upstairs and puts on a t-shirt and her shoes, before heading out the door. Stacey doesn't live that far away so it doesn't take Emma that long to get there. Approaching Stacey's house, she opens the gate and knocks on the door as quickly and as loudly as she can.

The door opens and Stacey appears. Seeing Emma looking flushed, Stacey asks what's up.

"Are you all right? You look like you've been running".

Looking slightly confused, Emma puts her hands on her hips and bends over to catch her breath. "You called me and told me to come over because you had something urgent to talk about".

Stacey invites Emma inside and closes the front door. Walking into the living room, Stacey asks what's going on. Emma explains to her that she called her about five minutes ago and told her to come over. Stacey picks up her mobile phone and shows Emma the phone log, which doesn't show any calls made for the last four hours.

They both sit down confused as to how it could have happened.

"It wasn't me who called you", Stacey says, frowning.

"Stacey I know your voice. It was you on the other end. I think we'd better go check on Chloe and make sure everything's all right". Dialling Chloe's number, Stacey waits, but the phone just keeps on ringing.

"She's not answering. I think we should go over there and see what's up".

Stacey and Emma both quickly get up and make the short walk over to Chloe's flat. Walking quickly, they get to the front door and Emma starts knocking, hoping that Chloe's all right. The door opens on its own, much to the girl's confusion. Walking inside they get the biggest shock of their lives.

Chapter Twelve

"Is that what I think it is?" Dave says as he stares at the computer screen in front of him. "Laura can you enlarge the picture a bit please".

Laura presses a few buttons and the picture becomes larger. The spare room of Edith's house fills the screen. The picture has Jack on one side of the room, with Dave stood nearby. On the opposite side of the room stands a ghostly figure of what looks like an old man. With a patched jumper and trousers on, he looks to be staring at Jack with his hand in the air, seemingly reaching out.

"That must be Edith's husband Walter", Laura says quietly to herself.

Flicking through a few more pictures, the same ghostly figure can be seen in various parts of the spare room. It's the last picture that gets everyone's attention. The ghost of Walter Cook seems to be bending over and looking into one of the boxes in the spare room. The hut goes silent for a while before John speaks.

"Something must be in that box that he wants. Maybe that's why he's still hanging around. He must have unfinished business here".

Dave takes his small recording device out of his pocket and passes it to Laura, who connects it to the computer. After listening to the audio a few times, Jack thinks he can hear something in the background.

"Laura, play that last fifteen seconds back could you please". Laura plays the sound clip back to the group and turns up the volume. They all hear silence for a few seconds and then a muffling sound. It sounds somewhat like a human voice.

"Any idea what the noise is?" John asks as he pulls his chair over and sits next to Laura.

"I'm not sure John, but give me a few minutes and I'll see if I can clear the audio up a bit.

After ten minutes, Laura calls the group over as she takes the headphones out of the computer and off her head. "I think I've cleaned the audio up enough to understand what the sound is. I think you're all going to be shocked at what you hear".

They all gather around the computer as Laura once again press the play button. A faint muffling sound is heard, before the faint voice of an elderly man can clearly be heard over the speakers.

"Tell Edith I love her".
The sound of the audio muffles again, before the faint voice can be heard again.
"Help me find it".
The audio then cuts off and Laura stops the recording, before looking at the group. A calm silence fills the small hut before Laura speaks again. "I never thought I would ever find anything like this".
"I can't believe I just heard that", John says. "I have goose bumps all over my body".
"So do I", Dave and Jack say at the same time.

Dave gets out his mobile phone and dials Edith's number, hoping she's not gone to bed yet. After a few rings she answers, and within five minutes they're all in the van on their way to her house. Getting out, they notice the sun going down, so they hurry up and knock on Edith's door. After a minute of waiting, she answers the door with a little smile on her face. Letting the team inside, they all sit down in the living room and talk about what they've seen and heard.

"You mean my Walter is still here?"

"Yes, we believe he's still here. Can you think of any reason why he would come back after all this time?" Jack asks, leaning forward and putting his hands on his knees.

"I can't think of anything off the top of my head my dear".

"Can we take another look upstairs if that's all right? We won't be long", John asks, folding his arms showing concern.

"Of course you can dear, I'm not going to bed just yet. I might have a sneaky drink in a minute".
Together, the team walk upstairs, and as they get closer to the spare room the familiar smell of Walter's aftershave fills the air. Stopping outside the room, Laura smiles before she pushes the door open and turns on the light.

"All right, where was Walter stood in the photo?" Dave asks Laura, who takes the picture out of her bag that she printed out earlier, and holds it up in the air.

Holding it up at the front of the room, the unmistakable figure of Walter can once again be seen bending over the boxes, as if he's looking for something.

Jack walks over to the boxes and pulls out the one that Walter was looking in. The box contains a few Christmas decorations, a light bulb, a box of old playing cards and a little vanity case wrapped in a cloth.

Jack gently picks up the box and opens it up. "I think we should show this to Edith", he says, closing the lid gently.

Walking down the stairs, they walk into the living room to see Edith drinking a neat whisky. Stopping when the group walks in, she offers them a drink.

"No thank you, we're fine thanks", Dave replies, putting his hands in the air. Jack shows Edith the little vanity case. Much to her delight when she sees it.

"I haven't seen this for such a long time. I thought I had lost it", she says with a tear rolling down her cheek.

Opening up the small vanity case, she takes out a few photos that she passes to Dave. The photos are of her and Walter at various moments of their lives. A picture of her and Walter getting married, the birth of their children Alex and Joanne, and a loving photo of them holding each other on their fiftieth wedding anniversary.

"Wow, these are amazing", Laura says. "You really did love each other".

Edith wipes her tears away from her eyes with a white hanky before smiling. "Yeah we really did have a great life together". Putting her hand back in the vanity case, she pulls out a little box that contains her wedding ring.

"I was ill a few months back and had to stay in hospital. My family must have put these things in the spare room when they looked after the house".

Edith puts the ring gently back on her finger. As she does, the familiar smell of Walter's aftershave fills the room, putting a smile on everyone's face.

After Edith had made a cup of tea for everyone, and told them about her life with Walter, Dave decides it's time they made a move. Walking out the front door, Edith stops him.

"I just want to thank you for helping an old lady out. I miss my Walter, but knowing he's here with me makes me so happy".

As the team all get in the van, Dave looks towards Edith, who's standing on her door step waving. Stood next to her is the ghostly figure of Walter, also waving with a smile on his face. Waving back, the team drive away back to the hut.

After a short drive back to the hut, they all go inside and put the heater on, before sitting down and talking about what happened.

"We really made that little old lady really happy didn't we?" Jack says as he leans back in his chair.

"Yeah we did. She's led such a happy life hasn't she", John replies, taking a sip of coffee from a flask.

"Walter and Edith really did share something special. True love", Laura says to the group, smiling.

After a brief silence, Dave opens up his folder of possible cases and searches through them once again.

"There's a haunted school a few miles away we could look at. What about the long stretch of road that people claim to have seen a woman dressed in her wedding gown hanging around, but disappears in front of them when they stop".

When Dave's finished speaking, Laura leans back in her chair and asks if they could investigate something a little different.

"What do you mean by different Laura?" John asks, turning the heater down a little.

"Well there's a huge mansion up on the moors that's been empty for years. It's believed to be haunted, that's why no one has purchased it".

"Seems like something worth looking at if you want", Dave replies, as he puts his notes in the drawer under his desk. We'll meet here tomorrow morning around ten, and then we'll make our way up there".

They all agree and walk out to their cars. John and Dave drive away into the distance, leaving Laura and Jack standing next to their own cars.

Before Jack can drive away, Laura walks up to his car, leans against the door and asks him to wind his window down. Winding it down, Jack notices Laura wants to say something but hesitates.

"Is everything all right Laura?"

"Jack, I want to talk to someone about what's going on, but I also don't trust anyone".

"Laura you can trust me. Tell you what, come over to mine and we'll have a good old chat about things".

Agreeing, they get in to their cars and drive away. Laura following behind as she doesn't really know where Jack lives. Pulling up outside his house, she follows him inside and sits down in the living room. Passing her a beer, he sits opposite and asks her what she wants to talk about.

"You know Jack I'm not really a bad person. I might seem like I'm being horrible to you, but I don't really mean it. I'm just a little stressed that's all".
"Stressed in what way?" Jack asks, sipping his beer and leaning back in his chair.
"I have a terrible home life, and an ass for a boyfriend".
"Why is he an ass? Doesn't he treat you very well?"

Laura sits forward, finishes her beer and explains what her boyfriend Alan has been like since he moved in with her.
"He's a slob, he just lays about drinking beer and eating pizza all day. He makes me do the washing, cooking and cleaning and doesn't move a muscle trying to help. It drives me mad".

"Does he have a job?" Jack asks, staring at an unhappy Laura.
"He used to work in a warehouse but he lost that job, and now he just hangs around the house and goes to the pub all the time".

Jack stands up, walks to the kitchen, and gets another couple of beers. Passing one to Laura, he sits back down and puts his beer on the floor in front of him before looking at his friend.

"You want to know why he treats you like he does?"

Laura takes a sip or her beer and nods her head as she leans back in the chair.

"Because you let him. With the way you shout at me sometimes I'm really surprised he pushes you around. Stand up to him and show him you're not afraid of him".

Laura smiles and looks to the ceiling before looking back down at Jack. "You know you're right Jack, I shouldn't let him push me around. It's my house, and if he doesn't like the way things are he can leave".

"That's the spirit. Now finish your beer and I'll get you another one", Jack replies, giving a thumbs up to Laura.

After a few more beers and a lot of laughing, Laura asks Jack what his story is.

"Well I grew up around the Plymouth area with my family, but moved to Exeter when I was about ten years old. I moved back down to Plymouth when I was eighteen and have lived here ever since". Laura smiles and finishes her beer. Throwing it in the bin near her, she stands up and stretches. "Time for me to go home I think". Standing still, she looks at the door, but seems rooted to the spot. She looks at Jack then back at the door.
"I don't want to go home to that slob. He makes me miserable".

Jack stands up and puts his hand on her shoulder. "You can stay on the sofa tonight if you want. We'll sort this mess out tomorrow morning".

"Thanks Jack. You're not such an idiot after all", she tells him with a smile.

Jack disappears upstairs and comes back down with a few pillows and some sheets. Passing them to her, he smiles and starts walking up the stairs. Stopping halfway, he leans over the railing and looks at Laura.
"If you want to talk about anything…."

Before he could finish his sentence, Laura interrupts him. "Thanks Jack. I really appreciate you doing this".
"No, I was going to say, if you want to talk about anything, can it wait until the morning, because I need my beauty sleep", he says, looking serious but failing.

Laura smiles and throws a pillow towards the stairs. "Night Jack", before turning off the living room light.
Jack lay staring at the ceiling for a while before drifting off to sleep. Downstairs Laura lay on her side staring out of the window. Unable to sleep, she walks up to the patio doors and unlocks them. Walking

out into a chilly garden, she sits on the wall with her arms wrapped around herself to keep warm. Staring up at the sky, she wonders what went through Paul's mind as he killed his wife and hung himself in his own bedroom. As the breeze starts to pick up she walks back inside but stops suddenly.

"What if Paul and his wife were murdered?" She says quietly to herself, before walking inside and locking the door behind her.

Chapter Thirteen

"Look at the state of this place. Everything's been turned over",
Emma says, shocked, with her hand over her mouth. Stacey stands
behind her wide-eyed at the mess in front of her. Chloe's flat has
been turned upside down. Chairs, tables, photos, cups and saucers
and all sorts of bits and pieces cover the floor. Walking through the
mess, Emma shouts for Chloe, hoping she's all right.

Stacey follows close behind. Walking into the living room, they push
a few chairs away hoping to see Chloe, but she's not anywhere in the
living room. Walking quickly upstairs, Emma and Stacey start
shouting her name, hoping she'll answer. Coming to the top of the
stairs, they see a few plants tipped over on the floor and a couple
towels thrown around the landing. They both seem to be drawn to
Chloe's bedroom.

"CHLOE YOU IN THERE?" Stacey shouts at the door.

With no answer, Emma pulls the handle down and starts to open the
door. As it opens they see the same kind of mess as outside. Clothes
and cushions and DVDS everywhere. With the bed on its side,
Stacey spots Chloe lying down in the corner of the room. Rushing
over, she checks for a pulse as Emma calls for an ambulance.

Stacey finds a blanket and puts it over Chloe, as she tries to keep her
warm. Five minutes later the medics arrive and take her away,
leaving Stacey and Emma alone in the flat.

"What do you think happened here?" Emma asks, looking around at
the mess in the living room.
"I have no idea what happened here. It looks like a tornado hit this
place", Stacey responds.
After tidying up a few things and straightening the tables and chairs,
they both head for the hospital, hoping Chloe's going to be all right.

After waiting at the hospital for forty-five minutes, they get told that they can go and see Chloe now, who's in a ward sitting up in her bed looking confused. Upon seeing her friends she smiles and waves them over.

"I'm over here", Chloe says from her bed.
Seeing their friend, Stacey and Emma give her a huge hug, before sitting down next to her. Staring at Chloe, Emma asks what had happened to her.
Taking a sip of water, Chloe pushes her hair behind her ear and recalls what she thinks happened earlier.

"I was just doing some bits and pieces after leaving Emma's flat, and my mobile phone rang. I answered it, and on the other end was Ben".
"What do you mean Ben was on the other end? You mean a friend of yours?" Stacey asks, folding her arms in her chair.
Chloe looks up as her smile disappears. "No. The Ben who was killed outside your house".

As Emma leans forward, she drops her bag on the floor. She bends down to pick it up, but when she gets back up she notices the ward is suddenly empty and deathly quiet. No patients in beds, no doctors or nurses anywhere. Even Stacey and Chloe have disappeared. Just an empty bed is in front of her. Standing up a little confused, she looks around the ward.

"What's going on? Where is everyone?"

Walking towards the door, she looks around the room once again before peaking outside into the corridor. Not seeing anyone around, Emma walks down the corridor nervously, not quite sure what's going on. Hearing voices ahead of her around the corner, she moves quickly, trying to hear if she can recognise any of them.

"Hey, I'm lost can you help…." she says as she turns the corner.

Stood in front of her is Stacey. As Emma walks towards her, Stacey's face turns from smiling, to being in pain in an instant, as she screams and falls forward onto her face. Staring at her body,

Emma sees a knife stuck in her back. Screaming loudly she starts running in the opposite direction. Turning around she runs straight into Chloe, who she nearly knocks over.

"Watch where you're going Emma, you could have hurt me". Standing up, Chloe puts her hand behind her back and smiles at Emma.

"I have a present for you".

Looking completely confused, Emma asks her friend what she has behind her back. In one swift movement, Chloe lunges forward and pushes Emma against the wall with one hand, while a knife in her other hand flies across Emma's throat.

Screaming loudly, Emma looks up to find she's sit sat in the hospital next to her friends.

"Are you all right?" Chloe asks. "You don't look so good. Actually you look really pale".

"I'll be all right, don't worry", Emma replies as she and Stacey say their goodbyes to Chloe and leave the hospital.

Driving home, Stacey notices Emma hasn't said much at all during the short journey home so she puts a reassuring hand on her knee and asks if everything is all right.
"Why don't you come over to mine and we'll talk about what happened", Stacey says with a reassuring smile.
As they approach Stacey's house, Stacey slows down and parks her car nearby. Walking towards the door, Emma notices Chloe walking past the garden and down the road. Looking at Stacey a little confused, they both go after her down the road.

"CHLOE WAIT!" Emma yells after her friend.

Chloe turns the corner a few yards ahead of her friends. Walking quickly around the corner, Emma and Stacey are shocked to see that nobody is there. Looking left and right, they can't see Chloe or anyone else anywhere. The street is silent and completely empty.

"Where did she go?" A bemused Stacey asks. "She couldn't have gone far, she was only a few yards in front of us".

Nodding, Emma agrees. Taking her mobile phone out, she starts dialling, but realises quickly that she can't phone Chloe, as she's still in hospital.
"Well, she isn't here anywhere, and we can't get hold of her on her mobile, so I suggest we get inside before the rain comes".
As they walk back around the corner, Stacey gets a feeling someone's watching her, so she stops in her tracks. Spotting something out of the corner of her eye she turns around quickly, but whatever it was has disappeared.

"You all right?" Emma asks. "You look a bit panicky".

"I'm fine. Come on lets go", Stacey replies, walking on ahead.

Approaching the door, Stacey and Emma stop suddenly when clouds start forming quickly in the sky above them, as the rain starts pouring down at a ferocious pace. Unlocking the door, they walk in quickly and shut it behind them. Standing in the passageway, Stacey looks around in shock. She doesn't recognise the house she's standing in.

"This isn't my house. What's going on?"

"What do you mean it's not your house?" Emma asks, confused. "This IS your house".

"No it isn't". Stacey responds, just as a fog starts to seep up from the floor beneath them.

Chapter Fourteen

Jack wakes up early in the morning, has a wash and wanders downstairs to see if Laura is awake.

Walking into the living room, he notices Laura bent over doing stretches. He leans against the door frame and watches her for a while, before he decides he'd better not stare for too long.

"Have a good sleep did we?" Jack asks, still leaning against the door frame. "I had as good a sleep as you can have on a sofa", she replies, stretching her arms out to her sides. "Thanks for a good laugh last night. You really cheered me up".

"No problem Laura, any time. You go home and clean yourself up because you smell, and we'll meet at the hut around ten if you want", Jack says with a serious look on his face.

"Hey I don't smell you cheeky sod", Laura replies, putting her arm in the air and sniffing herself. "Well I don't smell THAT bad".

Saying her goodbyes, she gets in her car and drives back home, but as she approaches her house her good mood changes. She knows as soon as she walks through the door, Alan is going to boss her around. Standing outside her front door, she takes a deep breath and walks inside.

"I'm home Alan", she mutters, walking into the living room. "Are you here?"

Not hearing anything, she walks upstairs and checks the rooms. Not finding him anywhere, she takes her clothes off and starts to have a shower. Feeling the water run down her body, she smiles and feels relaxed for the first time today. After taking her shower, she eats a little breakfast and checks her emails, which normally involves deleting a load of rubbish.

She answers a few text messages and throws away some of the mail she doesn't want. Hearing her mobile phone ring, she answers it and is surprised to hear a police woman's voice on the other end, asking Laura if she can pick up her boyfriend Alan, who was detained all night for being drunk and disorderly. Agreeing, she says she'll be there as soon as she can.

After a fifteen-minute drive to the police station, Laura parks her car outside and walks into a deserted reception area. A slim looking older woman appears from a door behind the desk and asks Laura if she can help in any way.

"My boyfriend Alan Jefferies was detained last night for being an ass, and I've come to bail him out, again".

"Let me just check the records miss", the receptionist says in a calm but stern voice. "Oh yes Alan Jefferies was detained for drunk and disorderly at ten thirty last night".

After waiting around for a while and sorting out various pieces of paperwork, Laura waits in the car for Alan. Appearing from the police station looking his normal scruffy self, he opens the car door and gets in.
"So are we going to talk about what you've been up to then?" Laura asks Alan, who just stares straight ahead.

"Wait until the guys in the pub hear about this, I'll be a hero", Alan mumbles under his breath with a grin.
Laura just shakes her head and drives back towards home. As she nears the street where she lives, Alan mutters for her to pull over.

"Why are we stopping?" Laura says, looking confused.

Alan starts to get out of the car but turns around and looks at Laura, grinning. "I'm going to the pub now to tell the guys about my night of being locked up, bye".

Without even saying thank you, Alan wanders off down the street into the local pub. Laura sighs loudly, before quickly driving off to meet Jack at the hut.

Jack sits in the hut alone for a while until an angry Laura stomps in and throws her bag down in the corner.
"What's up with you?" Jack asks, with his arms folded, sat in his chair. "Sit down and have a drink".
"I don't want a drink. I want to get rid of that lazy boyfriend of mine".

Jack sits up takes a sip of his coffee. "Just tell him to get lost then. Kick him out on his ass. So why the sudden anger towards him this morning?"

"He got himself arrested and spent the night in a cell. From what I heard he was shouting and swearing at anyone who was nearby. Eventually he got detained, so I had to bail him out this morning".
"Laura I want to help you get rid of him, but I think this is something you have to do on your own", Jack tells her in a serious tone.

"Yeah I think you're right. But enough about my private life, where have John and Dave got to?"
Just as Laura finishes her sentence, Dave rings Jack and tells him that he and John are going to do a case on their own for couple of hours.

"Well it looks like it's just you and me checking that old mansion out", Jack says as he stands up. "Dave and John are doing a small case on their own together".

Laura picks up her bag and walks towards the door. Putting her hand on the handle, she turns around and looks at Jack.
"Thanks for your advice about Alan", before walking out of the door.

Laura gets in her car and follows Jack to the location of the mansion, leaving the noise of the city and the constant traffic queues behind her. Crossing a small bridge that links the city to the outskirts, she takes in the scenery and vast open fields to her left and right. Horses, sheep, cows and goats chew on the grass without a care in the world. After ten minutes of driving, she sees Jack indicate and takes the next left, over the cattle grid and through a road between some trees. Driving for a little while, Laura spots a house coming into view in the distance. Stopping behind Jack, she waits for him to open a gate before driving through. Getting out herself she closes it again, before following Jack to the front of the mansion. Parking the car next to Jack's, she gets out and stands next to him.

In front of them stands a huge mansion that's seen better days. Moss growing up the walls and overgrown grass around the sides. A garage sits a few metres from the mansion with paint peeling from its door.

Jack takes a piece of paper out of his pocket and passes it to Laura.

"I did a little research on the mansion earlier. Turns out it's been stood like this for at least fifteen years. No one is willing to pay what is being asked for it, so it just stands here doing nothing. The building itself has stood for something like seventy years or so".

"Well let's go check it out then shall we?" Laura replies as she walks on ahead.

They walk up to the front door, at which point Jack gives it a little push that opens it almost straight away.

"You know this is classed as unlawful entry", Laura says, a little concerned.

"I know, but we're not doing any damage are we. We're just taking a look around".

Laura pushes the door open and they both walk inside. They stand on a marble covered floor. A grand foyer with two large stair cases greet them either side that ascend to the upstairs that are then joined in the middle by a long corridor. In-between them on the ground floor, sits two doors at the foot of either stair case, and a door on each side that make up the foyer.

"Wow, this place is huge", Laura interjects as her voice echoes throughout the foyer. "Time to take a look around".

They walk straight ahead through a door that leads to a huge dining room with a long table stretching from one end to the other.

"The ceiling is so high up, glad I'm not the one painting it", Jack says, staring up at the ceiling.

Laura bends down and looks up the chimney in the fireplace, but doesn't see much because it's too dark. Jack takes a few photos of the dining room, before they move on to the next room. Pushing the door open, they walk into a living room with chairs covered by spider webs, and tables covered with dust. Jack walks over to the window and looks outside. He sees his and Laura's cars parked nearby, and a forest in the distance.

"So does this mansion have much of a history?" Laura asks, sitting in a chair, putting her feet up on a table in front of her.

"From what I read on the internet, a few people who have lived here have died under strange circumstances", Jack responds reading from a piece of paper. "Up to about nineteen fifty-seven, as many as six residents have either just vanished, or committed suicide inside this mansion. Then after nineteen fifty-seven the suicides just stopped suddenly, everyone else who lived here led normal lives".

"Wow, sounds really strange, any idea why the suicides stopped?" Laura asks, standing up and wiping dust off of her jeans.
"I had a look, but couldn't find any reason why they just stopped. They just did".

Laura takes a few more pictures of the living room before they decide to move on. Trying one last room before they leave, they walk up the large stair case and into the foyer, and then stand on the landing overlooking the foyer below.

"What a fantastic view", Laura says as Jack takes a few more pictures. Turning around and walking down a corridor, they open a random door and walk inside. The room has a few boxes, a light swinging from the ceiling, and bits and pieces scattered all over the floor.

"Well there doesn't seem to be much in here does there", Jack says, taking a few photos.

Laura walks across the room to pick something up but suddenly trips and falls against the back wall. Hitting it quite hard, she screams as her shoulder hits the plaster. Jack quickly moves across the room to see if she's all right.

"You all right Laura?"

"Yeah I'll be fine. Can you help me up?"

Helping Laura to her feet, they look at the wall that she has just hit.

"You fat sod, you just put a hole in the wall", Jack says, laughing.

Laura laughs as she pushes Jack playfully in the arm. In front of them is a small hole in the wall, about the size of a fist. Jack takes out his torch and pears into the hole. As he does so, a huge rush of air comes out of it, causing both Jack and Laura to stand back quickly. Hearing a noise outside in the corridor, they look at each other and decide it's time to go. Walking out into the corridor, they start moving quicker, as a moaning sound can be heard coming from somewhere nearby. Laura runs out of the door, followed by Jack who pulls the door shut behind them.

"Let's meet back at the hut and see what we have", Jack says as he takes one last look back at the house before driving off, with Laura following closely behind.

Chapter Fifteen

Stacey and Emma stand by the front door of what should be Stacey's house, but everything is different, almost like they've gone back in time. Walking around what should be the hallway, they see an old woman dressed in a cloak waving some sort of sharp stick in the air, mumbling some kind of incantation from the living room.

"What's she saying?" Emma asks, wide-eyed. "I have no idea", Stacey replies as she moves forward into the living room.

The old woman's voice starts getting louder and louder as the two girls get closer to the room. As they get to the door, they can see something moving just out of sight against the wall in the living room. The old woman points the stick in the air with both hands before bowing her head and going completely silent.

In one sudden movement, she thrusts the sharp stick forward to the sound of an almighty scream. As Stacey and Emma move further into the room they see the stick embedded into a man's chest. With his hands and legs tied to posts, he continues screaming in agony. The girls look on in shock at what they've just witnessed.

Suddenly turning her head quickly towards them, the old woman pulls the sharp stick out of the man and points it at them.

"How dare you interrupt the sacrifice", she mutters in a slow, pained voice.

Stacey starts backing away, followed by Emma. The old woman walks quickly towards them and lifts her hand above her head. Stacey puts her hands up to protect herself, but as she does a bright flash of light fills the room.

As the girls take their hands away, they realise their back in Stacey's house. Looking around, Emma puts her hand over her mouth and starts walking out the door.

"I'm not spending another moment in here".

Stacey watches her friend disappear out the door, but decides not to follow her. Instead, she stands afraid in her house, looking around and wondering what's happening to her and her friends.

"I think I'm going to seek some proper advice", she says aloud to the house.

After a restless night without much sleep, Stacey gets out of bed. After sorting herself out, she logs onto the internet to see if she and find anyone who can help her find out what's been going on lately. After a few phone calls to the various paranormal teams around the area, which she's surprised there's so many, she finds a group of investigators who think they can help her out.
Sitting in her bedroom, she wonders about the last few days and what's happened to her and her friends. She didn't believe in the paranormal before, but after seeing what she's seen she has no doubt that something is out there.
Arriving at a creepy looking hut near some woods, she knocks on the door a few times before a man answers and invites her inside.

"So what can we do for you?" Dave asks, sitting back down in his chair behind his desk.

Stacey isn't sure what to say, as the subject of the paranormal is always something that people laugh at. But not sure who else to turn to, she tells Dave what's been happening to her and her friends.
"I've seen things. When I say I've seen things I mean my friends and I".

Dave leans back in his chair. "You've seen things? Like what? Ghosts? Spirits? Things going bump in the night?"

Stacey, looking sheepish, responds in a panicky voice. Her hands shaking and her eyes darting around the hut every so often. She explains the hand that grabbed her in the shower, the strange woman she saw when her house changed to another time and the word *'die'* that keeps appearing all the time.

Dave starts chewing on his pen, before he starts writing a few things down on his notepad in front of him. "Why would these things be happening to you and your friends? Have you done anything to anger them?"

Stacey looks at Dave and starts to say something but stops. "I got some candles and a few friends and…"

Dave looks Stacey in the eyes. "You used a Ouija board didn't you".

Stacey looks down at her lap "Yeah we did". Looking back up quickly, she shakes her head. "We didn't realise all this would happen. We just did it for a laugh". She puts her face in her hands. "None of us are getting any sleep, and we keep hearing and seeing all sorts of things. Dogs go mad when we're near them. It's been a nightmare".

Dave stands up, walks over to Stacey and puts his hand on her shoulder. "We'll do everything we can do to help you out".

After Stacey has left the hut, Dave writes a few things down and puts the paper in his folder. At that moment, Laura walks in followed by Jack a few moments later.

"Hey Dave, how's it going?" Jack asks. "How did your case go yesterday?"

Dave stands and picks up his bag, as he has to leave and finish the case he started yesterday.

"An old woman thinks she can see things moving at night, so I'm just going to do a follow up and see if anything had occurred last night. I'm on my way to pick up John. How did your visit go to the mansion?"

"We did find a few interesting things that we're going to look into", Laura tells him. "We'll explain more later".

With that, Dave leaves the hut and drives off to meet John.

Chapter Sixteen

Laura puts the memory card from the camera into the computer and waits for it to load as Jack starts making the tea. The computer fires up and a few pictures come onto the screen. Passing Laura her tea, Jack sits down next to her.

"Let's take a look at what we've got then", Laura says as she skims through the pictures. She stops at a picture and enlarges it. The picture of the wall with a small hole in it that Laura fell against fills the screen.
"I really think we should go check that out later", Jack says, drinking his tea.

Laura pushes the chair away from the desk. "We both heard strange noises in that house. Do you think we should really go back?"
"Yeah of course we should go back. I reckon there was a room behind that wall, and it might have something worth looking at".

After finishing their tea and sorting a few things out, Jack and Laura get some things together and head for the mansion. A few minutes later they're both stood outside the mansion once again. This time they know where they're going, so they head straight up to the room with the hole in the wall. Jack takes out his torch and shines through the hole.

"What do you see?" Laura asks with an anticipation.

Jack turns around and smiles. "Wonderful things".

"Well we can't go inside, there's no door or entrance or anything. It seems like this plaster wall was put up on purpose", Laura questions, looking around the room.
Putting his bag on the floor, Jack opens it and takes out a hammer and starts banging around the hole.

"Jack stop! You can't go into mansions and start knocking down walls". Before Laura could say anymore, Jack had made a hole big enough to climb into. "You can stay here if you want, but I'm going inside".

Jack picks up his bag and squeezes through the hole. Waving his hands around in the air, he waits for a little dust to disappear, then he turns on his torch.

"Found anything?" Laura asks over his shoulder.

"Don't do that", Jack says as he nearly jumps out of his skin. "I'm feeling jumpy today for some reason".

Waving their torches in front of them, they find a room full of boxes, shelves, a desk with chair and all sorts of things neatly placed against the wall in front of them. Laura spots a few candles and decides to light them all, causing the room to be enveloped in an orange flickering glow. They walk around in silence, picking up various objects and taking photos of everything they see.
Jack opens a large casket and smiles at his find.

"Hey Laura this is interesting. Well, if you're a science fiction fan anyway. There seems to be loads of old reels of English science fiction from the sixties and seventies".

"That's amazing", Laura says excitingly. "People have been searching for these all over the world and they're right here in England".

Laura walks away and opens a couple drawers full of jewellery and pieces of string. She looks at the wall in front of her, and spots a creepy looking painting of a middle-aged man sat in a chair.

"His eyes seem to be following us", Laura says, tilting her head to the side.

Jacks walks over and stares at the painting as well. "You're right they do seem to be staring at us. Creepy".

Laura opens another drawer and finds a shiny gold amulet with a few symbols on it. She starts to pick it up, but for some reason she stops and looks at Jack, who's busy taking photos of a map he found on a piece of paper. She turns back around, picks up the amulet and holds it in her hand. As she does, a gust of wind passes her and makes the candle flames flicker, causing Jack to look up and face Laura.

"Is everything all right?"

Laura puts the amulet in her bag. "Yeah I'm fine. I'm just amazed at this room that's all".

Jack picks up a few things and takes a few more photos before deciding it's time they left. Climbing through the hole again, they leave the room quietly and walk towards the large staircase.

"*Stop*", Laura whispers as she puts a hand on Jack's shoulder. "I think I heard something downstairs".

They both find a room and quickly dart inside. Laura turns around and is immediately surprised at what she sees. An old projector with a reel of film still in it, sits quietly facing the wall behind her. Walking over to it, she tries to switch it on but it doesn't have any film in it. Walking around to the front of the projector, she hears a crack and nearly falls over. Taking her foot out of the now cracked floorboard, she spots something wrapped in a cloth. Opening it she sees it's an old film reel. Wrapping it back up she quickly puts it into her bag as she sees Jack waving at her to hurry up. She zips up the bag before joining Jack at the door.

"Do you hear that?" Jack asks quietly. "Sounds like children laughing and playing".

Hearing the children coming closer, Jack closes the door just enough so he can see outside. The noise of the children playing and laughing passes the room, but he doesn't see any children. As the noise fades away, Jack looks at Laura and counts down from five. As he reaches two, Laura jumps up and bolts into the corridor.

"Laura wait!"

Starting to panic, she looks behind her, hearing all sorts of noises coming from all directions. Walking quickly down the stairs, she feels something grab her foot. Starting to fall, she feels another hand grab her arm.

Turning around she sees Jack smirking, who pulls her towards him. "You should be careful in old mansions like these. They can be dangerous".

Laura breathes a sigh relief. "Thanks Jack, you're a lifesaver. Now come on, let's get out of here before something else happens".

Walking down the stairs quickly, they close the front door behind them before getting in their cars. Jack drives off, leaving Laura to sort herself out before she goes. Taking a quick look back at the mansion, she sees a figure in the upstairs window staring down at her. Without wasting any more time, she starts the car and drives away as quickly as she can.

They both arrive back at the hut at nearly the same time. Going inside they sit down and relax and talk about some of the things they've heard and seen in the mansion.

"Jack I definitely saw someone in the top window as I was leaving".

"It could have been anything to be honest. Although we did hear voices on both the times we went into the mansion", Jack replies. "So what was on the amulet you picked up? Anything interesting?"

Laura takes the amulet out of her bag and passes it to Jack. "I'm not sure what the symbols are or what the writing says. We'll have to do a little research on that I think".

Jack gets out a magnifying glass and looks closely at the amulet. Writing down a few of the symbols he looks up at Laura, who's taking some of the things she picked up from the room out of her bag.

"I have a few things in my bag that could interest you".

Laura walks over, takes Jack's bag, and puts his finds on a table. Standing with her hands on her hips she looks at Jack. "We have all sorts of interesting things here don't we".

Jack stands up, walks over to the table, and nods. "Yeah, we certainly have".

As they're looking at the objects, John walks in the door and walks straight up to the table.

"What have you two been up to while we've been away then?"

"Ha-Ha very funny John", Laura responds, laughing. "We've been doing a little exploring in an old mansion. Shame you couldn't come along. You would've loved the place. So where's Dave?"

"He left before me, he should be here by now though. I'll give him a call".

John calls Dave's phone but gets no answer. "I'm sure he'll be here in a minute. So what do you have here then?"
"We have some reels of old film, but they're pretty useless without an old projector to play them on", Jack says, picking a few of them up.

John looks at his friends and raises his eyebrows. "I have an old projector at home. I'll bring it in and we can all have a movie evening together, as long as you guys bring the popcorn".

Chapter Seventeen

Emma relaxes in her flat on her own. After what she saw yesterday she wants a little time to herself, although she could have been a bit nicer to Stacey rather than just run out the door. With her phone turned off and her door locked, she sits in her living room alone, watching the television while having a few drinks.

Looking up, she sees a face she recognises on the television. Staring at her without blinking his eyes is Ben. An evil smile comes across his face as he points at Emma.

"You killed me Emma; you're going to pay the ultimate price".

Suddenly jumping up, she realises it was just a nightmare. With sweat on her brow and her hands clammy, she leaves the room to freshen herself up, unaware of the pair of eyes following her from the television screen behind her. Casually walking up the stairs, she walks into the bathroom and washes her face with cold water. Jumping suddenly when she hears the door slam behind her, the shower turns on at full blast. Backing up against the wall she sees a figure start to materialise in front of her. Panicking, she screams as loud as she can, she then finds herself frozen to the spot, just as the dark shadow gets closer. She then sees the bathroom door fly open. The shadow quickly disappears in front of her eyes.

Standing in front of her is Stacey. Looking confused and shocked, she puts her arms around her friend.

"What's happening to us?" Emma asks with tears streaming down her cheeks.

"I don't know Emma, I really don't know".

Stacey decides to go and visit the paranormal investigator she spoke to, while Emma sees if she can stay with her parents for a while until everything has blown over.

After driving nervously for bit, Stacey finds the hut where she met an investigator called Dave a while back. Getting out of the car, she knocks softly on the door. She puts her hands in her pockets as it seems colder than usual outside. After waiting for a minute or so, she starts to open the door, but as she gets close, the door opens and a young woman appears and asks her what she wants.

"I'm sorry to intrude, but I'm looking for Dave", Stacey says nervously. "Is he about?"

Laura looks at the girl suspiciously before inviting her inside. "No he's not about at the moment, but you can come in and tell me why you're here".

After making Stacey a cup of coffee and giving her a blanket to keep herself warm, Laura pulls up a chair in front of her and asks her what the problem is and why she wants to see Dave.

"My friends and I have had a few problems with the paranormal of late, and Dave said he would help us out. Hasn't he mentioned it to you?"

"No Stacey he hasn't mentioned it. We sometimes do our own cases, but if they get too intense we ask the rest of the group for help".

Stacey takes a sip of her coffee and explains everything that's been happening to her and her friends to Laura. After ten minutes of letting it all out of the bag, Stacey starts to sob. Laura gets up and puts her arm around the girl sat in front of her.

Bending down in front of Stacey, Laura smiles and takes her hand.

"We'll do everything we can to help you out. What you've been through is terrible. I can't imagine what it's been like for you and your friends".

Stacey wipes the tears away from her eyes and smiles. "I've heard of people who've seen ghosts, but never thought it would ever happen to me".

After talking for a bit, Laura tells Stacey she'll discuss what to do with her team when she sees them again, and then she'll get back to her when they decide what they're going to do. After watching Stacey leave, Laura sits staring at the door for a minute. She turns back to the computer and starts doing a little research on the amulet she found. At that moment, Jack and John walk in with a few bags an old projector in their hands.

"Hey Laura, look what I found in the attic", John says, putting the projector on the table. "Has Dave got in contact with you yet?"

"No he hasn't called or anything. I tried his mobile but it just kept ringing. Maybe we should go to his house tomorrow morning and see if he's at home".

John looks at Jack and nods his head. "Yeah we'll give him some time, then we'll try to find out what's happened to him".

John sets up the old projector, puts the reel on, and then presses play. Laura and Jack move a couple chairs over, sit, and wait for the show to start.

"How old is this projector?" Laura asks.

John sits back down and looks at Laura. "My mother's mother gave it to us many years ago. We put it in the loft and completely forgot about it until recently".

The projector hums to life and after a few seconds of scratching, a film reel countdown fills the screen.

The image of some children fades into focus as they run up some stairs in a big mansion. The same mansion Laura and Jack have visited on two occasions. The black and white flickering screen changes from one scene to another until it rests on a corridor. Where there are three little girls giggling and laughing together. Suddenly they stop playing and stand up, looking at each other before looking at a door down the corridor.

Jack looks at Laura and John who seem mesmerised by what they are seeing. Jack looks back at the screen and continues watching.

The three little girls walk slowly towards the door. Holding hands, they open it and walk inside. The lack of sound on the film make it difficult to know what's going on. After a minute of staring at a door, the camera pans down to see something trickling from underneath it that looks a lot like blood. The camera suddenly shakes and disappears behind some plants as the door opens. Out steps a well-dressed man with a hat on his head. Looking left and right, he rubs his hands on a cloth and throws it back in the room, before walking down the large stairs and out of the front door. The screen goes black for a few seconds before returning to a hand on the door. The black and white screen flickers left and right with scratches, that make it show its age.

As the hand pushes the door open, the room comes into full view. Much to the horror of John, Jack and Laura.
Laura puts her hand over her mouth at the scene in front of her. The bodies of the three little girls lay in the middle of the room. The camera moves closer, but suddenly shakes and falls to the ground. The scene in front of the camera makes Jack turn away briefly and look at John.

"I think we should turn it off now", John says nervously.

In front of the camera is the hand of a little girl holding a bloodstained doll. John, Jack and Laura all jump when a large boot fills the screen. Then the film goes black and ends.

"Where did you say you found this reel of film?" John says, taking the film off the projector.

Laura stands up, puts her hair behind her ears, and looks at John. "We found it under a loose floorboard when we were hiding from the sound of children laughing and playing in the mansion". She suddenly stops and puts her hand over her mouth and looks down. "Those noises we heard must have been of those poor little girls".

Laura logs onto the internet, and after a little searching finds a list a few pictures of the previous owners of the mansion. Clicking through a few, she stops at one certain picture. Jack stands there with his arms folded next to John, not quite sure what he's looking at.

"It's the same picture as the one we saw in the room", Jack says. "What's his name?"

Laura reads out the name next to picture.

"His name is James Harwood. He's also the person we saw walking out of the room where the girls were killed".

"I think things are really starting to get a bit weird don't you think?" Jack says with his arms still folded.
"Yeah I think you're right", Laura says, looking at her watch. "First thing tomorrow, we're going to go over to Dave's house and see where he's been. Then we're going to help out Stacey and her friend, because they really need our help".
John and Jack agree and they all go their separate ways. Into the darkness of the night. But before Laura leaves, Jack asks if she's going to be OK going back home.

"Yeah I'll be fine Jack, don't worry. Thanks for your help in all of this", Laura says before driving off into the night.

Chapter Eighteen

As morning comes, Jack wakes up to the sun shining, but disappearing behind some clouds every few minutes. After messing around a little too long getting ready, he meets John inside the hut followed by Laura a few minutes later. As they're discussing today's plans, Dave walks in calmly and sits down. Much to the surprise of the others.

"Where have you been? We haven't seen you for days", Laura asks, looking surprised to see her boss.
"What do you mean where have I been? I just left the house that John and I were investigating. Why are you all looking at me funny? What's going on?"

Laura walks up to Dave and stares at him. "That was over a day ago".

They all look at each other and walk over to Dave. Jack then pushes Dave's arm gently, much to Dave's annoyance.

"It is me you know. I'm not some kind of ghost".

They all sit back down and try to figure out what's going on. Dave sits at his desk while looking at the rest of the group, hoping their all playing a trick on him.

"The last thing I remember was finishing the case with John, and him driving off ahead of me. I followed him a few minutes later and came right here. I don't recall missing any time or anything".

Dave sits at his desk, not sure if he's hearing things right. He then puts his hand in the air and tells his friends to be quiet.

"John, what was the case you and Dave went on together?" Jack asks. "Anything that would suggest this would have something to do with the missing time Dave's experiencing?"

John starts explaining the case they went on together a few days ago. "We got a call from a middle-aged woman saying she keeps seeing a dark shadow at night, so we decided to go and investigate. After spending some time in the dark, we couldn't see anything like a shadow or figure lurking anywhere, so we told her to call us if she sees anything else.

She didn't seem to like that and wanted us to stay all night, to which we politely declined. As we were walking out of the door she started mumbling all kinds of weird and strange things as well as waving around some kind of wand. We just ignored it and got into our cars and headed back here".

"From what you've told us, I think she may have put some kind of spell on you", Laura says looking concerned.
"Wait a minute", Jack replies, smiling. "Are we seriously suggesting that this little old woman put a spell on Dave that caused him to miss time?"
The group look and each other, then back at Dave, whose sitting confused at his desk.
"Don't ask me, I haven't got a clue what's going on here".

"All right I think the best thing to do is carry on as normal and deal with any problems as they arise", Laura says in a commanding voice. "Everyone agree?"

"So what have I missed in my absence?" Dave asks, nervously.

Laura explains her and Jack's visit to the mansion, and the amulet she picked up. Dave picks up the amulet and looks at it under a magnifying glass.
"These symbols are very old. They could have come from anywhere. Where did you find it?"

"I found in it in a drawer with some other things behind a wall", she responds, looking at Jack. "There were lots of other weird and odd things in there, but we decided to only pick up a few things before we left the mansion".

Standing up and passing the amulet back to Laura, he sits back down and ponders the amulet for a second. "I've seen those symbols before but I can't quiet remember where though at the moment.

"We also found a reel of film", Jack says to Dave. "It's not for the faint of heart though".

After watching the reel of film, Dave looks at the rest of the group as he stands up and takes it off the projector.
"Should we hand this to the police?" Laura asks, looking at her boss.

"I think we should look into who the girls are first. Were they reported as missing at the time? What happened to the man you told me was James Harwood? How old is that reel of film, and are there any more lying around in that mansion?"

"Well I suggest we all get together later and figure this out", Dave tells the group, sitting back down at his desk. "I have a few things at home I need to sort out first".

"Are you going to be all right Dave?" Laura asks as she walks out the door. "I'll be fine don't worry", he replies as Laura closes the door behind her.

Laura, John and Jack all leave together and drive off, leaving Dave on his own in the hut to think about all that's happened over the last few hours. Putting his hands over his face, he leans back in his chair and sighs loudly. After a long hard think, he decides to visit the mansion on his own and get a feel for the place. After quick a drive, he arrives at the mansion. Standing outside, he stares up at the huge mansion in front of him. Looking back towards the gate, he decides he's come this far so he might as well carry on. Opening the door, he walks straight into the massive foyer to the sound of flapping birds echoing throughout.

He notices straight away that the place hasn't been lived in for a very long time. Stopping every few minutes, he takes various pictures of the rooms he walks into. Finding another winding corridor, he continues until he spots what looks like a light coming from the bottom of a door. Slowly walking forward, step by step, he puts his hand on the door and gives it a little push. A bright light immediately flows from the room, forcing him to shield his eyes. As he closes the door behind him, the light becomes dimmer and his eyes start to focus on his surroundings.

He finds himself in a single dark room, with a projector switched on in the center with an old style film reel countdown. The reel countdown seems to be stuck on the number three, so Dave gives the projector a shove. The counter starts counting down, and when it reaches zero, a garden comes into view. The camera slides quickly through the garden and then through a door on the side of a mansion. Dave looks around the room, but only sees one door behind him. Continuing to watch the film, he starts getting a little nervous and starts walking backwards towards the door. He then stops as he seems mesmerised by the film he's watching. The camera moves up a winding staircase and quickly across a landing, before stopping outside of an open door.

He walks forward and stares at the screen as the camera moves into the room. Dave stands rooted to the spot as he sees the back of a figure. His eyes widen as he realises the back of the figure he's staring at, is that of himself.

Chapter Nineteen

Emma wakes up to a quiet flat once again. She stares up at the ceiling and smiles. She doesn't know why she's smiling, she just is. Getting changed, she checks some things on the internet before walking to the shop to get a few things. She bumps into a woman on her way, who she hasn't seen for a while, who she used to babysit for a few years ago.

"Hi Mrs Landel, how you doing today? I haven't seen you around lately".

"I've been busy doing this and that and keeping my husband in check. Always breaking something he is. He broke a finger the other day putting a fence up".

"Wish him the best from me won't you", Emma says as she enters the shop. After buying a few things, she wanders back to her flat and puts them away. As she does, she receives a text message from Stacey telling her that she's going to pick up Chloe in an hour.

Sometime later, she gets in her car with Stacey and they drive away to the hospital, Unaware of a face staring at them from the kitchen window of Emma's flat.

After spending some time talking to doctors and nurses, Chloe picks up her things and finds Stacey and Emma stood by the car outside the hospital.

"It's so good to see you", Stacey says as she hugs her friend.
"How you feeling?" Emma asks, also giving her friend a hug.
"Much better thanks, a bit of a headache, but I'm sure that will pass in time".

They all get back into the car and head for Emma's flat for a few drinks and to talk over everything that's been going on. As they sit down in Emma's flat, Stacey asks Chloe how she's really feeling now she's back home and out of the hospital.

"I'm feeling fine thanks. Glad to get out of the noisy hospital and people rushing around everywhere".
"Well we're both glad your home", Stacey says, cheerfully. "It's been a testing time for all of us".
The mood dampens when Emma asks Chloe what happened to her to cause her to pass out the way she did.

"My mobile phone started ringing, and when I looked at the caller ID I didn't recognise the number, but I answered it anyway, thinking it was a friend or something. It turned out to be Ben. The guy who died the night we used the Ouija board".

"What did he say to you?" Stacey nervously asks.

"He said I killed him, and I'm going to pay", Chloe replies, folding her arms as she leans back in her seat.
"I had the same thing happen to me", Emma responds, much to the surprise of her friends.

"He said the same thing to me in a dream I had when I dozed off in the hospital earlier".

The room goes silent for a minute for so as the girls get themselves together, but the silence is broken by Stacey's mobile ringing loudly. After a brief conversation she hangs up the phone and explains who it was to Chloe and Emma.

"The paranormal team I've been talking to want to come over and talk to all of us, and then will hopefully end this hell we've been going through lately. They say that they might have a way to stop all these noises and shadows that we all keep seeing".

The girls all look at each other and smile, before Emma stands up and extends her arms to her friends. "Hopefully we can all get back to normal", she says, hugging her friends.

After a while, Emma gets up and answers the door to a woman and two men who then invite themselves in and sit down in the living room.

"I'm Laura, this is Jack and John, and we're here hopefully to help you get rid of your ghost problem".
"What are you going to do?" Chloe asks, taking a mouthful of coffee. Laura also takes a mouthful of her coffee, then she puts it back down on the table before leaning forward and putting her hands on her knees and looking between the three girls. "You're not going to like what we're going to do, but you have to trust us".

"Do you have any ideas that you think will work?" Emma asks quietly, a little concerned.
"We're going to have to use the Ouija board again", Jack says, looking at Stacey and her friends.

"NO WAY, I'M NOT DOING THAT AGAIN!" Chloe shouts, pointing her finger at Laura, before walking out to the kitchen.

John looks at Jack, who looks at Laura, who stands up, picks up her bag, and starts to walk out the front door. "All right then, if you don't trust us, then deal with it your own way. Come on guys lets go".

Jack and John follow behind Laura as they walk out of the flat.

"PLEASE, WAIT!" Stacey shouts as she runs after Laura. "You have to understand it was the Ouija board what caused all this trouble in the first place, so we're a little scared to use it again that's all".

Laura looks at Jack and smiles. "Shall we get started then?"

Standing in the living room, Laura explains what they have to do.

"Because the three of you didn't close the Ouija board session down properly and were interrupted by Ben, the spirit of something got out and is making your life hell. Ouija boards are not toys and shouldn't be played with as such".

The three girls look at each other and stand up. "What do we need to do to stop this?" Stacey asks, fidgeting with her hands.

"We need to do exactly what you did on that night, and close it down properly after. That might help, then again it might not", John says sternly. "Out of interest what did the spirit say to you? Did it spell out a name or anything like that?"

"I think it said its name was James Harwood, and he died in 1957", Stacey replies.

"That name rings a bell with me for some reason", Laura replies, rubbing her chin.

"We saw a gravestone with the name James Harwood on it, who died in 1957 just a few days ago when we went on that little camping trip together", Stacey replies quietly. "Could just be a coincidence though".

Jack, Laura and John look at each other, all thinking the same thing, but deciding to keep it to themselves for now.

After discussing what they'll need, Jack sets up the Ouija board, places the candles around the room, and dims the lights. They all sit around the Ouija board and hold hands and try to clear their minds of any thoughts.

The sound of faint breathing can be heard as the candles flicker around the room. After a few minutes, the pointer on the Ouija board starts shaking on the table, much to the amazement of Jack who's never seen anything like this before in his life. Seeing the board shaking, Laura starts calling on the spirit of James Harwood.

"I call on the spirit of James Harwood. Answer me if you're there".

After a brief pause, the pointer starts moving around the table, spelling out the word '*YES*'

Stacey starts reciting a protection ritual that she remembers from a long time ago.

"I call upon all things good and pure, cleanse this place and its inhabitants. Rid us of all things evil. Rid us of this evil spirit".

The board starts shaking and the candles start flickering faster, objects begin to fall off tables and cupboards. Then a calm. Before a white light fills the room and everything goes quiet.
Laura releases her grip from Stacey sat next to her, before looking into her eyes and taking her hands in hers. "The spirit is gone. You now should be able to live in peace and without fear".

"Thank you, thank you, thank you", Emma squeals, throwing her arms around Jack, a little too excitedly. "We can't thank you enough for what you've done".

"Next time you decide to have friends over, I suggest having a few drinks or playing some board games", John tells the girls, as he lets go of Chloe and walks towards the door with Jack and Laura.
"Take care girls and behave yourselves", Jack says, smiling and waving as he opens the door to Laura's car.

On the journey to the hut, they talk about where Dave has disappeared to once again. Not showing up in the morning made them change their plans and help out Stacey and her friends, rather than look into the symbols on the amulet.

"He might even be back at the hut", Jack says, leaning forward from the back seat.
Coming to a stop outside the hut, there's no sign of Dave's car anywhere. They open up the hut and Laura slumps down into her chair.

"You OK?" John asks an exhausted Laura. "You look tired".

"It does takes a lot out of you, chasing the paranormal around you know. I don't see Dave anywhere around, here so I suggest we all take the rest of the day off and relax a little and come back tomorrow, refreshed and ready for another day".

Chapter Twenty

Laura wakes up around nine o'clock in the morning after having a decent night's sleep for once. Staring at the ceiling, she smiles and bounces out of bed, totally forgetting that Alan isn't lying next to her. After a quick shower, she walks into the kitchen and makes herself some toast.

"Make me some breakfast", Alan moans from the living room. "I'm hungry and need food. Make it now".

Laura starts putting toast into the toaster then stops suddenly, before smiling to herself. After making her own breakfast, she wanders into the living room and changes the channel on the TV that Alan was part watching, as he takes another swig from his bottle of beer.

"Hey I was watching that, and where the hell is my breakfast?" Alan asks, sitting up to the sound of beer cans falling on the floor.

"I didn't make you any", Laura tells him as she eats her toast. "Make it yourself".

Alan looks left and right before standing up and towering over Laura, who's sat eating her breakfast and watching the TV.
She stands up slowly so she's face to face with Alan, and tells him how she feels, in a calm manner.

"Alan you're a lazy bastard who doesn't give a crap about me or anyone else. You live in MY house and have the cheek to order ME around?"
Alan stands back, not believing what he's hearing. Laura walks up to his face once again and stares at him straight in the eyes.
"I want you out of my house and out of my life for good. I'm giving you twenty minutes to get your things and get out".

After a few minutes of still being in shock, Alan grabs a bag and packs a few things before walking out of the front door. He turns around and starts to talk, but Laura slams the door in his face as hard as she can.

She walks into the living room and sits down. Looking at her hands she sees their still shaking. Looking up, she smiles and looks around her living room at the mess Alan has left for her. She bends down to pick up a can but suddenly hears a knock on the front door.

Standing up and putting her hands on her hips, she walks over to the front door and opens it. Concern turns to joy as she sees Jack standing there on her doorstep.

"Come in. You can help me clean up the mess my ex-boyfriend left me".

"You mean you finally got rid of that piece of crap did you?" Jack asks, folding his arms. "I hope you weren't too mean to him, he seemed like a decent guy".

"Decent guy? He was a complete ass and I'm better off without him".

"I'm only joking. He was a fool to treat you the way he did", Jack says, walking over and giving Laura a hug.

"Now, let's start clearing up this mess shall we", Jack says, throwing some cans in the bin.

"I can't be bothered doing it now", Laura replies, putting on her jacket. "I think we should get to the hut and see if we can find Dave. I'll message John on the way".

As Jack walks past Laura, she grabs his hand and stops him. "Jack you gave me the confidence to stand up to Alan. I just want to say thank you".

"Anytime you need someone to talk to or get drunk with, just give me a call all right. Now let's go. I'm kind of feeling a little scared at the moment".

"Why's that?" Laura asks.

"This is the first time I've seen the caring and soppy side of you. It's scary. Go back to being mean and nasty", Jack says, laughing as he gives Laura another hug.

She hits him in the arm as they walk to her car and drive off to the hut together.
Arriving at the hut, they open the door to find John sat in Dave's chair checking the drawers as if trying to find something.

"Is everything alright?" Jack asks as he stares at John from the other side of the desk.

John finally finds what he was looking for. "I was looking for the notes Dave kept on our visit to the cemetery a while back".
Laura sits down and messages a few people on her phone before looking back up at John, who's looking through the notes.

"I knew I recognised the name of the spirit haunting the three girls we just helped out", John says holding a piece of paper in the air.

"The name of the ghost they said was haunting them was James Harwood, who died in 1957. The name on the gravestone was the same name with the same date he died", John says wide-eyed.

"Do we know much about the guy besides him living in the mansion?"

Laura spins her chair around and puts the name James Harwood in a search engine and presses the enter key. A few searches come up with a few pieces of information. Laura clicks on a website and waits for it to load.

"Well it seems from what I'm reading here, James Harwood used to live in the same mansion we've been checking out, as we already know".

The website shows a black and white picture of James Harwood stood with his family and three young girls. After another search, Laura finds out the three young girls were James Harwood's sister's children. They disappeared but were never found.

The hut goes silent, as the team take in what they have just read. John picks up Dave's diary and reads it out loud. "Dave's last note he put on here was to check out the mansion. He managed to translate what the symbols said on the diary".

"What do they translate as?" Jack asks.

John looks up and stares at his friends. "It translates as the word *'die'*. How creepy is that?"

They all look at each other, before grabbing a few things and heading towards the mansion out on the moors.

Chapter Twenty-One

Stacey takes a bite of a donut and looks around the small restaurant she's having her lunch in. Smiling at the children, who are playing with their various toys and eating their dinner, while making a mess of it.

"Are you staring into space again Stacey?" Emma jokingly asks, sitting in front of her friend and waving her hand in front of her face.

"No I'm just glad all the crap we've been through is over now, and we can get back to living our lives again".
They both sit and look at each other, before Emma's phone starts ringing. After a brief conversation she hangs up and explains the call to Stacey.

"That was Chloe. She said she's just finished getting her hair done and she'll meet us here in a minute".

After talking about the future for a while, laughing, and joking about things they got up to when they were younger, Chloe walks in and does a little twirl, showing off her new hairstyle.

"I can't believe you've changed your hair colour to red", Emma says. "I'm jealous".

"So am I", Stacey replies, with a big smile, that spreads across her face. "It suits you".

"Stacey, did you believe in the paranormal before all this started with the Ouija board", Emma asks, drinking her coffee.
"To be honest Emma, I kind of had the feeling something was there, but never in a million years did I think it would happen to us. I wouldn't have done the Ouija board if I knew the trouble it would have caused".

"The main thing is we're all fine and have come through this stronger than we were before", Chloe says with a grin on her face. "I fancy seeing a movie, you interested?" She asks her friends.

"Yeah I think we could do with a bit of normality", Emma replies, picking up her bag.

"We might as well walk; it's only around the corner from here".

The three girls start the short walk to the cinema, laughing and joking as they go. Stacey bends down and strokes a dogs ears, much to its enjoyment. Walking on ahead, they come to entrance of the cinema and all walk in.

"I'm paying", Chloe insists, taking some money out of her bag. "My treat".

They all settle in their seats in the dark as the adverts play before the film.

"What film are we seeing anyway?" Stacey asks.

"I think it's some kind of romantic comedy with Jim Carrey and Jennifer Aniston". Chloe responds as she turns her phone off. Halfway through the film, Chloe decides she needs to go to the toilet, so she gets up and wanders off. "I'll be back in a minute".

Nearly ten minutes go by, and Stacey starts to get concerned about her friend. "She should be back by now. I'm going to go and find her".

A further ten minutes go by and neither Stacey nor Chloe have come back. Emma decides it's best if she tries to find them herself. Leaving the dark cinema, she covers her eyes as she opens the curtain at the far end, as the light almost blinds her for a moment. Standing outside screen five, she quickly notices how quiet and empty it is. Seeing the sign pointing to the toilets, she starts walking down a dimly lit corridor.

"Stacey you here?" She says in a panicky voice. "Chloe, where are you?"

Suddenly she hears a noise in front of her and starts walking towards it. She stops as she sees the lights flickering. Then notices Stacey stood at the far end of the corridor.

"Stacey what are you doing all the way back here? The toilets are at the other…"

Emma stops mid-sentence and stares at her friend, whose face is motionless.

"Are you all right Stacey? What's going on? Speak to me".

Stacey's face has no emotion; she slowly falls forward onto her face, much to the shock of Emma. Screaming at the top of her voice Emma spots a knife sticking out of Stacey's back. Quickly bending down, she holds her friends head in her hands as tears stream down her cheeks.

"Come on Stacey wake up". Panicking, she checks her friends pulse, but there isn't one. She hugs her one last time before gently putting her head back down on the floor.

"You can't be dead. This can't be happening. This must be a nightmare".

Emma stands up and quickly walks in the opposite direction. She quickens her pace but bumps into someone and crashes to the floor.

"Emma I'm so sorry I knocked you over", Chloe says, extending her hand.

Emma stands up on her own and stares at her friend who seems to have a creepy smile.

"Chloe, Stacey's dead, she has a knife in her back, I don't know what to do", Emma says in a screechy panicky voice. "What do we do?"

Chloe just stares at Emma, smiling. Noticing Chloe has one hand behind her back, Emma starts walking backwards.

Chloe quickly moves towards Emma and pushes her against the wall with one hand.

"Hey what are you doing?" A frightened Emma asks her friend.

"You thought you could get rid of me didn't you?" Chloe says quietly with an evil grin on her face.

"Didn't your parents tell you not to play with things you don't understand?"

"What are you on about Chloe, I don't understand what you're saying", as tears start rolling down her cheeks.
In one swift movement, Chloe swings her arm from behind her and slashes Emma's throat. Emma grabs hold of her bleeding throat as she slides down the wall and on to the floor. Her hands then go limp as they fall to the floor.

Chloe stands over Emma's body laughing, before she turns the knife on herself. Thrusting the knife into her heart, she gasps as tears come streaming down her face.

"I'm so sorry", she says, with her last dying breath, before she collapses onto the floor.

Chapter Twenty-Two

John, Jack and Laura get out of the van and quickly walk towards the front door of the mansion. John gives it a kick and it opens straight away.

Walking inside, Laura doesn't waste any time in shouting for Dave.

"DAVE YOU IN HERE!"

Jack and Laura run quickly straight ahead through a door between the two large staircases while John runs quickly up the stairs, shouting for Dave as he goes. He tries opening various doors, but most seem to be locked. He then comes to a door with a light shining underneath it. Gently opening the door, he sees Dave stood facing the wall in the far corner of the room.

"Dave what's going on? Why are you in here?"

Dave doesn't say anything, he just stands there completely still facing the corner. John walks over to him and puts his hand on his shoulder. Turning him around John falls to the floor in shock at the sight in front of him. Dave has no eyes, just holes where his eyes used to be, and his mouth has been sown up with stitches. Dave falls to ground, with blood dripping out of his eyes.

Then John jumps up, and runs for the stairs, looking behind him every few steps. He stops suddenly when he sees three little girls skipping towards him, laughing and playing. They stop and smile at him.

"The bad man is going to get you", one of the girls whispers, before they both skip away down the corridor.

"LAURA? JACK? WHERE ARE YOU?" He shouts down the echoing corridors.

John runs through to the top of the large staircase and stares down at the marble floor below.

"Can I help you young man?" A voice mutters from behind him. "What are you doing in my house?" Stood in front of John is a man dressed in a very old style suit and a top hat.

"Your house?" John says, confused. "Who are you?"

"I'm James Harwood", before smiling and pushing John over the banister onto the hard marble floor below. Killing him instantly.

"Did you hear that?" Jack says to Laura, getting to his feet. "It sounded like someone screaming".

"I didn't hear anything", Laura replies as she opens another door searching for Dave. "Well I don't think he's anywhere around here".

They both come to a small winding staircase that looks like it goes up a few floors. Jack looks up, but walks behind Laura. "I'm not going the up there first, you do it".

Laura stands there with her hands on her hips laughing at Jack. "You're such a wimp Mr Harrison aren't you. I'll go first then".

Laura starts walking up the dimly lit staircase one-step at a time with a giggling Jack following closely behind.

"What's so funny?" Laura asks as she begins to climb the stairs.

"Has anyone ever told you that you have a lovely bum?" Jack says, laughing.

"That's such a sweet thing to say Jack, and also a bit creepy", she says, giggling to herself.

They reach the top of the stairs and come to a half-open door. Pushing it gently, Laura opens it and walks out onto a landing somewhere in the middle of the mansion.

"Come on, let's try to find Dave and John and get out of here", Jack tells Laura as she shines her torch on various things on shelves in the corridor. Jack opens a door and is immediately shocked at what he sees. Laura puts her hand over her mouth in shock at the sight of Dave.

Lying dead on the floor in front of them, Dave has no eyes and his mouth has been sown up.

"COME ON WE'RE LEAVING NOW!" Jack shouts, running away. "Laura come on, we can't do anything for him". Grabbing Laura's hand, he runs with her down the corridor and into another room. Slamming the door, Jack turns around to see Laura with her hand over mouth crying. Walking forward he puts both his hands on her shoulders and looks her in the eyes.

"We have to be strong. Let's get out of here first, and then we can deal with what we saw in there. Ok?"

Laura nods her head up and down quickly, before walking away over to the dirty window on the other side of the room. Jack takes a quick look out to the corridor, before hearing a huge crash behind him. Turning around quickly he sees dust and pieces of wood everywhere, and a hole in the floor.

"LAURA, YOU ALL RIGHT?" He shouts down the small hole in the floor. Waving the dust away he sees Laura lying on the ground, completely still.

"I'M COMING DOWN!" He shouts. But gets no reply or movement whatsoever.

Once the dust has settled, he lowers himself down onto the rubble below him. Rushing over to an unconscious Laura, he picks her head up and wipes some dust away from her face.

"LAURA WAKE UP!" He shouts, as he gently starts slapping her face, trying to wake her up. "Come on Laura time to wake up. No time for lazing around".

Laura slowly opens her eyes to the smiling face of Jack looking at her.

"Jack what happened? The last thing I remember is falling through a hole in the floor".

"You did fall through a hole in the floor. Into this dusty old room underneath", Jack says, throwing bits of wood from on top of Laura. "Can you walk?"

Laura tries to get up but falls back down again. "I think I've busted my leg. Leave me here and go and get help".

"I'm not leaving you here on your own. Come on I'll carry you", Jack says as he picks up Laura and holds her in his arms. "Damn you're heavy. You should lose some weight when we get out of here".

"Firstly Jack, I'm not fat, just a little podgy thank you very much, and secondly, if you slap my face again, I'll kick your ass. All right?"

"I'm only joking. Come on let's get out of here".

They walk down a dimly lit corridor, past open doors, knocked over tables and plant pots. Jack carries Laura through into another room and puts her down on the floor, before sitting next to her and taking a break.

Laura looks at Jack, then puts her head down and starts fiddling with her fingers. "What's going on here Jack? What happened to Dave? I can't believe this has happened. All we do is investigate the paranormal. We don't cause any trouble. We're good people. Aren't we?"

Jack moves closer to Laura, puts his arm around her, and kisses her on the forehead. "Yeah we're good people. I don't know why this has happened to us".

Jack stands up again and helps Laura to her feet. Putting her arm around his shoulder, they walk out of the room and into the corridor. Jack leans Laura against the side of the corridor as she takes out her phone and calls Johns mobile.

"Wait, can you hear that?" Jack asks, looking left and right. "It sounds like Johns ringtone. Come on lets follow it".

Picking up Laura quickly, Jack walks fast towards the sound of the ringtone. Walking to the end of the corridor and onto the landing in the foyer, they finally see where the sound of the ringtone is coming from.

Chapter Twenty-Three

Laura buries her face in Jack's shoulder when she sees the dead body of John lying on the marble floor below. With a trickle of blood coming from his nose, and his eyes still open, he's completely lifeless.

Laura looks at Jack as tears start streaming down her cheeks.

"Come on Laura stop crying. You can cry for as long as you want when we're outside, but at the moment I need the hard face of Laura who scares the crap out of me every day".

Laura wipes her tears away and smiles at Jack. "Let's get out of here".

As they turn around, the sound of children laughing gets louder, and the three young girls walk up the stairs and stop next to Jack and Laura. With their smiles disappearing, one of them looks at Laura. "The bad man is coming".

The three girls giggle and then start skipping off into the distance. Suddenly a figure appears behind Jack, causing him to jump.

"What are you doing in my house!" he says in an aggressive voice. "I'm James Harwood and I deserve to be treated with respect!"

Laura is suddenly pushed over the landing. Jack reacts quickly and grabs her arm before she can hit the marble floor below.

"DON'T LET ME GO JACK!" She screams as she looks down at the floor below.

"I WON'T LET YOU GO!" He screams back at Laura who's panicking.

Looking up, Jack sees the ghostly figure with a large glass vase over his head mumbling all sorts of strange words.

"Jack I'm slipping, I can't hold on much longer".

Jack notices the figure has an amulet around James Harwood's neck, similar to the one Laura picked up from the room they broke into a while back.

"LAURA DO YOU HAVE THAT AMULET IN YOUR POCKET?"

"YEAH, I HAVE IT IN MY POCKET, WHY?" She shouts as she tries not to slip to her death.

"I WANT YOU TO TAKE IT OUT OF YOUR POCKET AND SMASH IT ON THE GROUND!" He shouts, hoping Laura hurries up.

Laura reaches into her pocket and grabs the amulet. Throwing it as hard as she can at the marble floor, she hears it smash into a hundred pieces. The figure swings the vase but instantly disappears, causing the vase to smash on the floor below, just missing Jack's head as it does so.

Jack quickly pulls Laura up onto the landing. Falling on his knees, Jack tries to catch his breath before looking at Laura.

"How did you know smashing the amulet would work?" Laura asks.

Jack looks at Laura and laughs. "I didn't".

"You mean I could have fallen to my death and you went on a hunch?" Laura moans as she's lying on the floor.

"Details, details", Jack replies as he stands up holding his hand out to Laura. "Come on let's get out of here shall we?"

Laura puts her arm around Jack and they slowly descend the stairs. Reaching the bottom they stop near the lifeless body of John.

"I'll call the police when we get home", Jack says quietly as they walk out of the front door, and into the bright light of another sunny day.

Epilogue

Four days had passed since Jack and Laura escaped from the mansion that took the lives of their friends John and Dave. Since finding out that the Stacey, Emma and Chloe were found murdered in a cinema complex, Laura hasn't spoken to anyone or answered her phone. She's stayed in her house and tried to come to terms with the last few weeks.

She hears a knock on the door but tries to ignore it. The knocking continues for two minutes until she gives up and answers it. Opening it she sees Jack stood there with a grin on his face, and some beer cans in his hand.

"Hello, I'm Jack and I was wondering if you could give me five minutes of your time please", he says, laughing.

Laura throws her arms around him and invites him inside. "So what brings you to my neck of the woods?"

Jack sits down and passes a can of beer to Laura. "I was just wondering how you're doing. I haven't seen you for a few days and thought giving you some space was the best thing to do".

"Jack I just want to thank you for helping me escape that mansion. I don't know what I would have done if you weren't there".

"Same goes for you. You're a tough cookie Laura. But there's one thing I'm slightly worried about".
"What's that then?" Laura asks, looking concerned and putting her can back on the table.

Jack leans forward and takes a deep breath. "You're turning from a hard-nosed bitch to a soppy old sock", laughing to himself.
       Laura laughs and throws a cushion at him. "Seriously though Jack thanks for everything".

"Anytime", he says throwing the cushion back. "So what are we going to do about the paranormal investigating business?"

"I'm not sure yet to be honest, I haven't decided if I want to carry it on without Paul, John and Dave. They were like family to me, you know. I'll give it a few days and decide if I want to carry on doing it".

"Well, if you do decide to keep doing it, give me a call all right", Jack says putting his can in the bin. "I miss John, Dave and Paul as well. I didn't know them as well as you but I still considered them good friends".

"Jack, the police told me something this morning that I'm a little confused and scared about".

"What do you mean confused and scared?" Jack asks, staring at Laura.
"They said that there were no bodies in the mansion. They couldn't find any blood or anything. John and Dave are considered missing persons at the moment".

"We saw those bodies Laura", Jack says quietly. "We lost good friends in that mansion".

"I know, I saw them as well. I don't understand", she says looking down at her knees.

After a brief silence, Laura pulls out a few pieces of paper from her bag and passes them to Jack. "I did a little research into James Harwood. He seemed to always be in the newspapers doing something or other. Stories of different women, the usual gossip from that era. There's a picture in there of him wearing the amulet we found. There's not much to go on but it seems he was very close to it for some reason".

"What about the three little girls we saw?" Jack asks, putting the pieces of paper on the table.

"They were never found. They went off playing in the woods but never returned", Laura tells him as she fiddles with the sleeve of her jumper.

"We have the old film reel showing them being killed don't we?" Jack asks getting concerned.

Laura shakes her head from side to side. "Nope, the police said they tried the film but the reel was empty".

"Laura what's going on here? Are we going mad or something, because I swear what I saw in that mansion was as real as you're sitting here with me now".

Laura looks at Jack and smiles. "We're not mad, well I'm not anyway but I do think we've been through something really strange over the last week or so that neither of us can explain".

Jack nods his head and stands up. "You want to go out and have something to eat somewhere? My treat".

Laura stands up and picks up her jacket. "Yeah I could do with some fresh air, I haven't been out for a while".

They walk out the door talking about where they want to go and what they'll eat. The front door closes and the sound of locks clicking fills the empty house. The silence is broken as the TV switches on, and a pair of eyes fill the screen for a few seconds, before disappearing into the darkness.

THE END

Message from the Author

Writing a book takes a lot of time, patience and effort. Once you start writing it you have to finish it. You'll go through hours of staring at the screen, trying to think of how to finish a chapter or if the dialogue fits right.

You'll be walking in the street or doing something at work then suddenly an idea will pop into your head and you're trying to find any kind of paper to write it down before you forget. This has happened to me many times.

You will lose count of the amount of times you read the whole thing through, or check that the spelling and grammar are done properly. With every book you write, you learn new ways to make things easier for yourself. From experience, I've learnt you can't rush a book out. You have to be 100% happy with what you've written. It could take six months to finish or it could take nine.
You could be happy with what you've written and ready to publish it, but suddenly you come up with something you want to add. That happened to me twice once I thought I was ready to publish this book.

I finished what I wrote and was happy with what I achieved. I printed it out and went over the spelling and grammar again and corrected any mistakes I could find. I put the finished copy down on the side, and left it for a week and carried on with my daily life, not thinking about it at all.
I came back and read it through again, and after not thinking about it for a week, I found I added or took away a few words or dialogues.

Every writer is different. Each have their own style and way of getting a story across to the reader. Some won't like what you've written, while others will love it. Writing can be hard, but I've learnt you have to take the rough with the smooth.

I'm sure throughout our lives, we've read books and not been happy with the ending or the death of a certain loved character, and thought we could do better. Sometimes that can inspire you to write your own piece of writing. Writing can be a lot of fun because you can write whatever you like without any boundaries.

My advice to anyone who starts writing any kind of book or literature, is to take your time and make sure you're happy before publishing it.

I would like to thank my friends and family once again for continued patience in completing this book. I've lost count of the amount of times they've asked me if I had finished yet, but all in good humour.

Without the support of my family I don't know if I would have finished this book. A big thank you to all of you.

Other E-books by this Author

Fear

AISN: B00FO7COC6

We're all afraid of something, whether it be spiders, heights or the dark. When teenager Sarah Jessop gets kidnapped, she learns first-hand what Fear is all about.

Trapped in a basement in the middle of nowhere, with seemingly no escape and a creepy figure stalking her, she has to learn about growing up the hard way and hope somebody hears her cries for help.

Printed in Great Britain
by Amazon

30319676R00076